THE BOY WHO LIED

Praise for Kim Slater:

'A remarkable first novel' *Guardian* on *Smart*

'It made me see the world in a different way' Ellen, age 12, for lovereading4kids.co.uk on *Smart*

'Kim Slater has struck gold again . . . a moving and uplifting novel' *School Librarian* on *A Seven-Letter Word*

'Pace, wit, pathos and humour in a book that looks and feels engaging' *Carousel* on *A Seven-Letter Word*

'Powerful and thought-provoking . . . Kim Slater's message on diversity is loud and clear' ReadingZone on *928 Miles from Home*

'[A] warm, truthful and insightful depiction of working-class life' lovereading4kids.co.uk on *928 Miles from Home*

'A fast-paced mystery with plenty of twists and turns but it's al~~so a heartfelt and powerful piece of social~~ comment~~~~

THE BOY WHO LIED

KIM SLATER

MACMILLAN CHILDREN'S BOOKS

First published 2018 by Macmillan Children's Books

This edition published 2019 by Macmillan Children's Books
an imprint of Pan Macmillan
20 New Wharf Road, London N1 9RR
Associated companies throughout the world
www.panmacmillan.com

ISBN 978-1-5098-4228-5

1 3 5 7 9 8 6 4 2

A CIP catalogue record for this book is available from
the British Library.

Typeset by Nigel Hazle
Printed and bound by CPI Group (UK) Ltd, Croydon CR0 4YY

To Lukasz and Liola with love
Both still too young to read my books but I hope
one day you will enjoy them xx

'Be yourself; everyone else is already taken.'

Oscar Wilde

This is what happened the day my brother went missing. It's all I can remember.

Me and our Sam went down Bulwell Bogs. We weren't doing much, just messing about and stuff.

This bloke walked by. He had a beard and looked a bit scruffy. He wore a checked shirt and his trousers were tucked in those wide-topped tan-coloured boots, like a builder. He looked at us, but he didn't say anything, and then he disappeared.

That's the only person I remember seeing that day.

I was sitting on top of the climbing frame, balancing on the two thinnest bits, when I saw our Sam talking near the swings.

At first, I thought he was just talking to himself; he does that a lot. But then I saw he was kind of talking into the bushes, like there was someone hiding there.

'Sam,' I called down to him. 'Come here. NOW.' But he ignored me, just carried on talking to the bushes.

I shouted again and this time he glanced up at me, and

I saw the bushes rustle and move like there was someone in there, watching us.

I yelled, loud as I could, 'Hey! What you up to over there?'

Our Sam is only eight years old and I'm not being rotten, but he isn't the sharpest knife in the drawer, if you know what I mean, and I was supposed to be looking after him.

But my brother didn't even turn round – he just stared into the bushes like a zombie.

And . . . and that's all I can remember. I don't remember seeing anyone, but there was this awful dread flooding through me, like I knew something terrible was about to happen to him.

That's when everything turned upside down, including Sam and the bushes.

I stretched my arms out to try to break my fall, but they just reached up towards the sky. I fell on my back and I think my head must've hit something hard because everything went black.

When I woke up, I was in hospital.

A nurse and a copper stood by my bed, and Mum was there too.

Her face was tear-stained and her hair looked all thin and greasy like it does when she hasn't washed it for a few days. Mum's best friend, Augustine, had her arm around her shoulders.

2

Charlie, Augustine's boyfriend, walked in and looked at me, and his mouth twisted up into a tight little knot, but he didn't say anything.

'What happened? Where's Sam?' I whispered to my mum.

'We think you must have fallen off the climbing frame in the playground, Ed,' Mum said, wiping her eyes. 'And Sam's gone missing. The police can't find him anywhere. Did you see anyone with him, Ed?'

None of them believed me. Not Mum, not Charlie. Nobody believed I really couldn't remember what had happened to my brother.

It felt like an army of ants was marching from my toes to my face and back again. The nurse told me to stop scratching; my skin was getting raw.

I wanted to cry like a baby, scream at them to listen, to believe me.

Because, for the first time in a long, long time, I was actually telling the truth.

DAY ONE

NOTTINGHAM POST

LOCAL BOY MISSING
Communities join forces

Yesterday, police praised Bulwell residents and the surrounding communities for their help in searching for missing 8-year-old local boy Samuel Clayton.

The boy, known to friends and family as Sam, went missing late on Sunday afternoon while visiting Bulwell Hall Park with his 14-year-old brother, Edward.

Due to an accident involving Sam's brother falling from play equipment, police say it is still not clear exactly how Sam went missing.

Within hours of his disappearance, community leaders organized a local gathering through social media, where over 200 volunteers took part in a three-hour fingertip search of the park and nearby woodland.

Police would like to question a bearded man of dishevelled appearance with light-brown short hair who was seen in the area shortly before Sam's disappearance. He wore a checked shirt and beige trousers tucked into tan-coloured boots.

Door-to-door enquiries and a wider search are expected to take place today.

Anyone who saw Sam at the park or who has any further information can contact Nottinghamshire Police.

It's the day after my brother went missing, and I am alone in a small white room.

My heartbeat is thumping in my throat and I feel sick and tired.

I can't hear the usual hospital-type noises or the hushed pad of soft shoes as the nurses dash about. Instead, there's a hum of frantic voices growing steadily louder outside the closed door. Someone shouts and then there's a scuffling noise.

A thump on the door makes my heartbeat blip. It sounds like someone just fell against it. I don't move.

I'm facing away from the door and lying on my right-hand side because it hurts to keep turning my neck. I think I must have twisted it when I fell. From here, I can stare out of the small window to the bushes beyond.

I've seen those kinds of bushes before; there are purple flowers on them that attract butterflies. We learned about plants in Biology during the spring term, but I can't remember the name of this one. Instead, I focus on trying to remember all the chemical symbols and the important dates in our history project, but all the facts feel chewed up together in my mind.

Still, it's better than thinking about why I'm here in the hospital. About what happened yesterday afternoon . . . Anything is better than that.

The noise outside dies down and then the door opens. I squeeze my eyes shut and pretend to be asleep.

'Ahh, admiring our lovely buddleia, I see.' I hear Dr Wood walk around to the bottom of the bed. 'You've got the best room here, you know. Best view, anyhow.'

I open my eyes again. Outside, the butterflies flit around, showing off like they know we're admiring them. I spot a couple of red speckled woods and a brimstone. And I'm sure there was a red admiral out there, just before I closed my eyes.

What does it matter?

'I'm sorry about the disturbance,' Dr Wood says briskly. 'Somehow the press got on to the ward. Very resourceful, they are. Turn up at visiting time, you see, and slip in with the genuine families.'

'Is Mum OK?' I ask.

When the two reporters and a cameraman had appeared at the door fifteen minutes ago, Mum had dashed out of the room, pale and panicky.

'We're from the *Nottingham Post*,' one of them blurted out urgently. 'Can you tell us what happened at the park yesterday, Ed? Do you often take your brother out alone?'

'Get out!' Mum had screeched. 'Isn't there any security in this place?'

Charlie pushed the photographer, who had said the F-word about ten times when his lens had slipped out of his hand and smashed on the floor.

Nurses and doctors had come running, and the quiet space had suddenly seemed very crowded and noisy. Through it all, the woman kept shouting questions at me. Then two policemen appeared and escorted the reporters out.

I pulled the sheet up over my head and waited until the sickly feeling passed.

Dr Wood stops moving and looks at me. 'Your mum is fine, Ed. The family liaison worker is with her right now, but she'll be back soon. Did you want me to call your neighbour Charlie in?'

'No,' I say quickly.

Dr Wood turns and plucks the clipboard from the bottom of my bed.

'I don't remember what happened at the park,' I say for about the hundredth time, my eyes prickling. I'm saying it as much to myself as to him. 'Honest, I don't.'

'You probably will regain your memory.' The doctor looks up from studying the paperwork. 'Sadly, it can't be rushed. It'll come back when it's good and ready and—'

'But what about our Sam? What if he's –' My voice cracks as I interrupt him and a tear traces down my cheek. I hope it gets absorbed into the pillow before Dr Wood notices.

'I know the police are going to be talking to you, trying to help you to remember, and that's important. Then you'll be in the best possible position to help your brother.'

I sniff.

'Good news. Your readings are nice and stable now.' He scribbles something on a sheet of paper and hooks the clipboard back on the bed rail. 'In fact, we can probably get you home later today.'

'Home?' I try to swallow down the lump that's just appeared in my throat, but it doesn't budge.

'There's no sense in you lying here bored out of your mind now we've checked you out. And I bet you'd much rather be comfy back at home on your Xbox, eh?'

He grins and winks, and somehow I manage a weak smile.

I think about our cold house, with its peeling wallpaper and draughty windows.

I think about how we've never had an Xbox.

I think about how we hardly ever even get to watch a full programme on the TV because the electric usually runs out before the end.

2

Jill, who's our family liaison officer, takes me and Mum home in an unmarked police car. Augustine has already gone back to the house so she can sort everything out there for our arrival.

Charlie left the hospital earlier to see his friend at the pub for a *business meeting*, he'd said. Seems he hasn't got the same worries about Sam as the rest of us, otherwise he'd be out there looking for him.

'My job is to take care of you and your mum,' Jill had told me when she first came to the hospital. 'You can talk to me about anything, but I won't be questioning you like the other officers. It's easiest just to think of me as a family friend.'

When she went to get Mum a cup of coffee, Charlie said we shouldn't trust her.

'Just keep quiet when she's around. D'ya hear me?'

But didn't the police need to know everything? How could they possibly find Sam if we didn't tell them all the facts?

I looked at Mum, waited for her to say something to Charlie, but she just stared at her hands again, chafing her sore index finger with a thumbnail.

At first, it was a bit weird, Jill being around at the hospital all the time, but after a while I forgot she was there. She's nice and friendly and she sort of melts into the background.

My head feels fuzzy with a dull ache that doesn't seem to get any better or worse. I only started taking the tablets Dr Wood prescribed me earlier today, though, and he said they'd take a while to kick in. It doesn't feel great, but I can put up with it. At least the sharp pains that felt like my skull was splitting in two have stopped.

'Fortunately, you didn't injure your head seriously when you fell off the climbing equipment,' Dr Wood told me. 'But stress and trauma can be responsible for very bad headaches. The pains should fade very soon.'

The ache in my heart when I think about my brother is harder to ignore. And it hurts far more.

When we're about halfway home from the hospital, I doze off in the back seat of the car. I'm dreaming of being on the climbing frame in the park again, with Sam.

This time, I don't fall and bang my head. Best of all, Sam doesn't go anywhere near the bushes.

'Bloody hell, what the—' Mum cries out.

I snap awake and nearly jump out of my skin.

'What's wrong?' I gasp.

The car slows right down and stops, and my mouth drops open when I see the street outside our house. It looks like a music festival is taking place. A great crowd of people rush forward when they see the car.

The men and women at the front have notepads and microphones and cameras. Behind them, I spot some of our neighbours, craning their necks to get a better look.

'Welcome to the circus,' Jill says, and then speaks into the radio, calling for a response.

I squeeze Mum's shoulder from behind, but she doesn't look round.

'Lorraine, Ed, don't get out of the car until the officers open the doors.' Jill flicks her seat belt off and twists round to face me in her seat. 'Ed, don't answer any questions they direct at you, love. At this stage, you shouldn't comment. Keep your eyes looking down and just allow the officer to help you inside. OK?'

I nod and glance at Mum. I'm not sure she's taking in what Jill is saying.

She's just staring out of the window at the flashing cameras, the desperate faces. They're all shouting at once, so it's impossible to catch anything they're saying.

Two police officers appear and the crowd falls back. One reaches for Mum's door handle, and another for mine. They open them at the same time and noise floods into the car like a tsunami of sound.

People clap and yell. Everybody usually ignores us around here. Now they all want to talk to us.

A strong hand grips my upper arm. The officer smiles

and says something, but I can't hear what. He pulls gently, placing a flat hand on my head until I'm safely out and can stand up.

I press my hands to my ears as the splitting pains I thought had gone begin again, shooting from behind my eyes, ricocheting inside my skull like red-hot laser beams.

Jill said to keep my eyes down, and I try, but it's hard to do. There are too many faces staring. Puzzled, angry, sympathetic. I've never seen most of these people before, but they all seem to recognize me.

'Ed . . . Ed . . . Ed,' all the different voices call out.

As we inch closer to our small, wooden front gate, I spot our neighbours Marg and Arthur. Their faces are lined with concern and Marg has tears in her eyes. Arthur gives me a thumbs-up, but he doesn't smile.

I see a flash of another one of our neighbours, Sylvester, and I wish I could talk to him, but then someone steps in front of him and he's suddenly lost in a sea of bodies.

'Ed . . . Ed . . . Ed!' All these strangers know my name.

'What did you see?'

'Why didn't you stop him?'

'Where exactly were you when Sam went missing?'

I don't answer, don't react, but it doesn't stop me feeling something spiky and sharp scraping the pit of my stomach.

They're asking the exact same questions as Mum and

the police already have. I didn't have any answers then, and I don't have any now.

A screech from the back of the crowd draws my gaze and I see a piece of card held up above all the heads. Written in thick, black ink are the words:

Mothers like Lorraine Clayton don't deserve kids

They're blaming Mum, even though she wasn't at the park with us. How can that be fair?

'Where were your parents while you were at the park?' a woman yells from somewhere at the back of the crowd.

I've been so busy trying to think what might have happened to Sam that I've lost sight of the real issue. My eight-year-old brother was in *my* care.

He's still at primary school and I'll be fifteen next month.

My job was to look after him – that's all I had to do.

Other people in my year look after their kid brother or sister all the time, so how could I have blown it so completely?

'Edward, do you think someone abducted your brother?' A woman thrusts a microphone at me and for a couple of seconds I freeze and stare into her face. She wears a concerned expression, but her glinting eyes look hungry, like a wolf's.

'No comment!' Jill snaps from behind me, and I feel her hand on my back, gently urging me to move forward.

My stomach contracts into a big, hard knot and it's then that the truth hits me.

Sam going missing is all my fault.

3

'Stand back, please,' says the leading police officer as he forges his way authoritatively through the crowd.

We walk down the short front path that's overgrown with weeds. Mum keeps saying she's going to do a bit of gardening to neaten up the front. She even said it the day before yesterday. When life was still normal. When I'd felt hard done by because there was no food in for supper . . .

I'd been irritated because we'd had to go up to our room early. There was nothing to do downstairs and Mum said she needed space.

I felt like there was rock music playing at top volume in my head. I paced up and down the tiny aisle in the middle of our beds. I just couldn't sit still at all.

Mum's not the only one. I'd like some space – probably Sam would too. But space is hard to come by when you're all cramped together in one room because the heating is off everywhere else.

I know Mum meant she needs space in her head to try and get the sad thoughts to quieten down. She's always like that when she's taken her tablets before bed. We try to be quiet and tiptoe around her, but sometimes she just wants us out of the way.

'Ed,' Sam said in his whiney voice, and I knew what was coming. 'I'm hungry.'

'You should be used to it by now,' I snapped.

Sam isn't as good at dealing with it as I am. He still thinks things will change if he whines enough, like food might magically appear in the cupboards.

'Ed,' Sam said again.

'Sam, just shut it, will you? There's nothing to eat. Live with it.' I felt the guilt, like a curl of smoke, unfurling inside me.

'Fine. I just wanted to talk – that's all.' He picked up his pillow and slammed it back down again before lying down and turning his back.

'Talk about what?' I sighed, still sorry for snapping at him. After pacing around, I suddenly felt like I could sleep for a week.

'I wanted to tell you about a secret. But it doesn't matter now. I don't want to talk to you.'

Sam and his silly secret that didn't exist. He was always babbling on about it lately, but he'd never actually said what it might be.

'Please yourself,' I said, and lay down on my own bed, staring up at a cobweb in the corner of the ceiling.

Sam fell fast asleep. I lay awake for ages on my

own, shivering under the thin quilt and listening to my stomach rumbling.

Our short path seems like the longest walk in the world, but, finally, I get to the front door.

The copper stands aside as the door swings open and Augustine ushers us all inside.

I walk down the hallway, a little apart from the others, and stand staring at the white wall in front of me. There are dirty fingerprints and scuffmarks on there. Sam always leans on the wall to put his trainers on.

The last police officer closes the door behind her as she steps inside the house, halving the volume of the shouting outside.

Augustine shakes her head. 'An hour ago there was nobody out there.'

'They'll have had a tip-off from someone at the hospital.' The taller officer frowns. 'No way of telling who it might be.'

'I'm Lorraine's best friend,' Augustine says to Jill and the two officers. 'Me and my boyfriend, Charlie, thought it'd be best for me to come round, to be here for them.'

'Thanks, Augustine,' says Jill. 'I think that's a good idea.'

Augustine and Mum look at each other. Mum's face is pinched tight, as if she's trying to stop any words from getting in or out of her mouth.

'They'll find him.' Augustine gathers Mum into her big, soft arms. 'It'll all be fine, you'll see.'

I scuff my toe on the wooden floor.

Augustine turns to me. 'How are you, love?'

'The doctor says his memory should come back,' Mum says in a small voice. 'If Ed can just remember everything that happened, then . . . we might . . . oh!'

Mum seems to collapse inwards like all her insides have melted away. She leans against Augustine and starts to wail, a horrible sound like she's being strangled.

'Where's my Sam? Where's my baby boy?'

She won't stop. She keeps crying out the same words, again and again.

My hands clamp on to my ears as a moving picture of Sam, walking towards the bushes at the park, replays in my head.

Why can't I remember more? Why didn't I stick with him, stay closer to him?

Invisible hands are choking me. I drag in air, but I'm still out of breath.

Jill rushes over, slides her arm round my shoulders. 'You OK, Ed? Breathe . . . That's it. Just breathe.'

One of the coppers gets me a drink of water and I gulp it down.

'Thanks,' I croak, handing him back the empty glass.

'A couple of detectives will be here to speak to you soon,' Jill says. 'Nothing to worry about – they just want a friendly chat. Why don't you go and rest for a while?'

I turn away and walk into the living room to sit down. I can hear the adults talking in low voices in the kitchen at the back of the house. Now I'm in here alone, I let my mask fall away. My throat feels sore, but my breathing is normal again. My lips lose their pucker and I close my eyes and rest my head back against the cushions.

It feels like all the important information the police need to help my brother is trapped behind a locked steel door in my head that even I don't have the key for.

If I try to remember the day leading up to that point, maybe there will be clues about who's taken Sam? I have to do *something*.

I open my eyes and wipe them with the back of my hand.

The last time I was here, in this room, Sam was with me. We'd just got our coats on to leave for the park . . .

4

Mum, Augustine and Charlie had been to the pub. I'd woken up in the early hours to their muffled laughter and stumbling about on the landing.

The next morning when I'd gone downstairs to make my and Sam's breakfast, I'd forgotten we had nothing in. No milk, no cereal and no bread. I knew better than to wake Mum up, so we'd ended up sitting in the living room looking at an old comic and sharing a small bag of crisps I'd found in the bread bin.

An hour later, there'd still been no sign of life from Mum's room, and Sam's belly had been rumbling again. Loud enough to hear over the other side of the room. I'd have to think of something good to take his mind off it or he'd set off on one of his unstoppable tantrums. If he woke Mum up, it'd be all my fault. It always was.

'Get dressed,' I'd said. 'We'll go kind-fishing up Bulwell Hall Park.'

Sam really liked it at the park. He caught sticklebacks and minnows with his green net. He put them in a jar and then threw them back in before we left. He called it kind-fishing because the fish don't get hurt. Sam has always been good at inventing new names for stuff.

'I'm hungry,' Sam had said when we reached the top of the hill that led down to the park.

My heart sank when I spotted the Flying Sausage, a food van that set up at weekends opposite Barker's Wood. Each step had brought us closer to the delicious smell of fried onions.

Sam had tugged at my sleeve as we entered the park.

'Ed, I'm hungry.'

'Yeah, me too,' I'd said, glancing at the food van. 'But we've no money to buy a hot dog, Sam.'

'What about a small burger?'

'No money for that, either. Sorry.'

'Arrgghh!' He'd started doing his giant temper steps, stamping his feet down really hard with each stride.

Sam had been seeing a therapist at school who was supposed to be helping him with his frustrations. That's how the head teacher had put it to Mum, anyway, when he'd called her into school for a meeting.

'It's just a fancy word for having a rotten temper,' Mum fumed when she got home. 'Have you ever heard such a ridiculous job title? Behaviour Management Therapist . . . pfft! Flipping do-gooders, the lot of 'em. None of 'em has a clue what a hard life looks like.'

Sam pulled on my sleeve again.

'Can you ask the lady, Ed?' He looked up at me, his face pained. 'Ask her if she'll give us a free one. Or just half of one.'

Sam expected people to help him – he didn't understand yet that some could be two-faced or mean. If people pretended to be nice, Sam just swallowed it, hook, line and sinker, like one of those sticklebacks in the lake.

I worried a lot about him getting bullied when he moved up to the comprehensive school and had to deal with people like Aidan Taylor.

We got level with the food van and I smiled tentatively at the lady cooking at the hot plate. She had an upside down, triangular face with sharp features that seemed to match the dangerous-looking pronged tool she stabbed the meat with.

'Go on, ask her,' Sam had whispered from behind his hand. His nostrils flared, dragging in the irresistible smell that had even started to get to me.

'Nah.' I steered him wide of the van. 'I've got something better we can do to make the hunger pangs go away.'

'What?' Sam scowled, unconvinced.

'Easy-peasy.' I grinned at his annoyed face. 'We dream.'

'Argghh!' He stomped off in front, shouting, 'I don't want to dream! I just want to eat something.'

I remembered what the head teacher had said to Mum about distracting him before he had a tantrum.

'Sam, wait! Do you want to be a policeman when you grow up?'

I knew he didn't want to be a policeman, of course, but it got his attention.

He turned round and punched his hands on to his hips. 'No!'

'Remind me again, then: what do you want to be?'

'A farmer,' he said slowly, as if I'd find it difficult to understand. 'A proper farmer with my own tractor.'

'Oh, yes, I remember now,' I said, picking up my pace to catch up with him as we passed the golf course on our right-hand side. 'What colour will your tractor be?'

'Red,' he said without hesitation. 'With massive tyres and a shiny black comfy seat where I'll sit and nobody else is allowed.'

At home, Sam's wall in our shared bedroom was covered in posters of farm machinery and vehicles.

'What else will you have on your farm?'

'A combine harvester. A yellow one.' His eyes were bright now, looking ahead as if there was one right in front of us.

'I always get confused, Sam.' I played along. 'Tell me again what a combine harvester does?'

'You are so stupid.'

I'd heard Charlie calling him that when Mum and Augustine weren't around.

'We don't use that word with each other,' I said softly. 'We're the smartest kids on the block. Remember?'

'You are stupid, though.' Sam raised his voice. 'I told

26

you before, Ed. A combine harvester collects up the crops. It reaps, threshes and winnows, and it combines them all into one.'

Sam's last school report said he had trouble focusing properly and didn't do well in his assessments because he found it difficult to retain information.

But I knew if they tested the whole school on farm machinery, Sam would come out top.

My thoughts are interrupted by sharp pains in my hands. When I look down, my fingernails are embedded in the soft flesh of my palms.

My whole body aches with wishing so hard that I could turn the clock back to Sunday morning and start over again.

5

I hear a phone ringing in another room. Jill's head appears round the living-room door.

'An officer outside just rang me, Ed. He says your friend Imran is in the crowd. He wants to come in for five minutes, if that's OK?'

My mouth is instantly dry. Imran is my only friend at school and I go round to his house all the time. But he's never been here, to my house.

I think back to last Friday at school when my biggest problem was staying out of Aidan Taylor's way.

'Ed!' Imran had beamed at me when I got to school that morning. 'All right?'

'Yeah, I suppose.' I shrugged.

'Look, I brought cake.' He opened a canvas bag and I caught a waft of sweet sugar. I'd had no breakfast. I had this crazy urge to snatch the bag and tear open all of the small, neat napkin-wrapped squares.

And then I remembered.

'Happy birthday,' I said smoothly. 'Bet you thought I'd forgotten, but I overslept this morning. I left your card and present at home.'

28

He looked away and smiled. 'It's fine, Ed. Don't worry about it.'

I narrowed my eyes.

'It's true, you know.' The words dripped effortlessly from my lips. 'I went into town specially to get your present earlier in the week and I know you're going to love it. Soon as I saw it, I knew it would be perfect for you.'

'Wow . . . thanks,' he said. 'I can't wait to see it.'

I couldn't tell if he was being sarcastic or not.

'The card I got is brilliant too. I'm so mad I forgot to bring them today, but I'll remember tomorrow. Promise.'

Part of me wanted to stop before I dug myself in any deeper, but I couldn't. I never can.

'I could come to your house after school if you like,' Imran said, brightening suddenly at the idea. 'Mum's doing me a bit of a birthday tea, but not until six o'clock when my aunties and uncles get there. And she says you're invited.'

'Oh! Great, thanks.' The cogs in my head began whizzing round. 'Except I'm not going home after school, so you can't come over tonight.'

'Where you going?'

'To . . . the doctor's. My foot has been killing me.' He watched as I limped around in a circle. 'Mum made me an appointment for today.'

The smile slid from Imran's face. 'I guess I'll just

have to wait until tomorrow, then.'

His voice sounded flat. I hadn't got any birthday treats for him, but some stupid part of me thought I might be able to get something in time for tomorrow. It felt like the truth.

'It'll be worth the wait.' I grinned. 'You'll see.'

He stared down at his feet.

'Did you get new trainers?' I asked him.

'They're a bit more than trainers. Proper Jordans, these are, man.'

He moved his feet this way and that, admiring the buff black leather and the glittery gold wing on each side.

'They've got Air Zoom and everything.'

'They're awesome,' I said, glancing down at my old school shoes. They were so scuffed, the toes looked grey now, not black. 'You'd better make sure Mr Skelton doesn't spot them.'

Our head teacher is hot on school uniform. He prowls the corridors and outdoor courtyards at every opportunity, scouring the school premises for offenders.

But Imran is clever. His designer clothes are never flashy enough to draw attention, and he always sticks to the official school colours, but his clothes and shoes often have a little Jack Wills or Nike logo here and there.

'Who cares.' Imran pulled a face. 'My mum says she'll sort it if there's any trouble.'

Mrs Javeed is a human-rights lawyer who works a

couple of days a week in London. She's also the chair of governors at Bulwell Park Academy and sent Imran to a state school on principle. Nobody messes with Mrs Javeed. Especially not Mr Skelton, who turns into a quivering wreck whenever he sees her.

'These Jordans were over four hundred quid, so I'll be wearing them now, whatever Mr Skelton says.'

I looked down at the Jordans. The gold wing shone under the fluorescent strip lighting.

They were just trainers . . . but, somehow, they said a lot more than that. They gave Imran a bit more swagger, proved nobody could tell him he didn't fit in.

Four hundred pounds.

They turned our electricity off a month ago because Mum didn't pay the bill. It was a hundred and twenty pounds. She had to agree to have a meter installed and now we pay for the electric on a card before we even use it.

'So.' Imran nudged me. 'Whadaya think?'

'They're awesome.' I nodded. 'Really awesome.'

'Thanks.' He grinned. 'I know you're not really bothered about this kind of stuff.'

That was how Imran and I played it. It saved having to talk about how we had no money and they did. Somehow, it allowed us to stay friends despite the different worlds we lived in when we left school every day.

6

When Jill tells me that Imran is outside, I start to feel itchy all over.

I've been to his house with his huge bedroom full of all the latest virtual-reality gear, but he's never been here. I've never invited him to come in.

'So I'll say he can see you. Is that OK?' Jill smiles.

'I – I'm not sure,' I falter. 'I feel a bit tired and—'

'Come on. It'll do you good to see a friend in the middle of this madness.' She nods at the crowd outside the gate. 'Talking to someone you trust might help you get through, Ed.'

Before I can answer, she steps back into the hallway and I hear the front door open.

The crowd noise ramps up a notch and the reporters and cameramen cluster closer to the gate. The door closes again and I hear Jill speaking in a low voice.

Then Imran appears in the doorway. His mouth hangs open as he looks around the room. He's probably aghast at the peeling wallpaper and our outdated chunky television.

'Ed!' He walks over and sits in the other chair, perching on the edge of the cushion like he might not stay long. He nods outside. 'Jeez, man. This is, like . . .

32

crazy. What happened? I mean – where do you think Sam went?'

'I don't know,' I say in a tone that hopefully tells him I don't want to discuss it.

'So, this is your place, then? Someone from school told me they live near you and said there's a massive crowd outside your house. Didn't take long to find you.' He's staring at the burn on the carpet where Charlie fell asleep drunk and knocked a candle over.

'This is not where we live most of the time,' I tell him. 'We're only here temporarily.'

He looks at me. 'Yeah? Why's that?'

I pause for a moment and press my lips together to try not to speak, but the words still manage to force their way out like they always do.

'We're having a posh house built . . . It's ten times bigger than this one.'

Imran shakes his head. 'Ed, it's OK. You don't have to—'

I speak over him. 'Me and our Sam are getting our own bedrooms and a games room with a big screen on the wall, like yours.'

'Cool,' Imran says slowly.

'We're gonna have a door between our bedrooms, and then if Sam feels scared in the night, I can look after him and –' My voice cracks and I bite my fist to make it stop and squeeze my eyes shut to stop tears spilling over.

'Mate, it's OK.' Imran sits on the arm of my chair and puts his hand on my shoulder. 'It must be . . . really hard for you right now.'

It sounds like he's trying to choose the right words to say and isn't sure if he's managing it. But I can't back down now. I just can't.

In my mind I can see the big, new house so clearly. Sam, kicking back in a big padded gaming chair with crisps and pop. He's safe and happy . . .

I'm not ready to let the pictures go. I want so much for them to be real.

I blink to clear my bleary eyes and look at him.

'When the new house is built, Mum says—'

'Ed . . . just stop! Stop telling lies! I don't care where you live – I'm your mate.'

Silence. Then Imran speaks again, his voice softer.

'What happened at the park? To Sam? Is it true you can't remember?'

'I don't want to talk about it!' I yell at him, the blood whooshing into my ears.

'I can understand how upset you are, Ed, honest I can. But you've got to stop lying about things . . . If you can remember, you need to tell the police so—'

'Just go! Leave me alone,' I shout, and push him hard. He stumbles off the chair arm, only managing to get his balance at the last second.

'Fine!' he yells back at me. 'I was only worried – that's

why I came to see you. After what you'd said at school on Friday . . . Well, I wondered if it had anything to do with Sam going missing. That's all.'

He glares down at me.

'What?' The hot fury drains out of my face in an instant. I speak slowly, quietly. 'What did I say on Friday?'

'That you'd found something out that was worrying you. Remember?'

'No – I've been kind of confused. Is that all I said, that I was worried?'

'You said you thought somebody was watching your house. Can't you remember that?' He looks at me like I've lost my mind. 'When I heard Sam had gone missing, I thought that might have something to do with it.'

I glance at the living-room door, but there's nobody there.

'I said that?' I hiss. 'What else did I say?'

'That was it.' Imran frowns. 'You said you should be able to find out more over the weekend and that you'd tell me on Monday, at school.'

'I . . . I'm trying to think.' I close my eyes, but nothing comes.

'You really don't remember saying it?' He rolls his eyes. 'It might be important, Ed. You need to tell the police.'

I feel the colour draining from my cheeks.

'Can I ask you something? How can you remember

some things and not others?' He looks awkward. 'People out there, they're saying you might be hiding something. That you're telling lies and—'

'Why won't anyone believe me?' I snap, suddenly desperate to be alone. 'I don't want to talk about it. Maybe you should go.'

'Is everything all right in here?' Jill's worried face appears at the door. 'Oh! Are you leaving already, Imran?'

'Yeah, I know when I'm not wanted,' he mumbles, and doesn't look back before he heads out into the hallway again.

I hear the front door open and then slam shut.

Jill looks at me, but I turn away and stare out of the window, watching as Imran stomps down the path. He disappears into the crowd.

I shouldn't have lost my temper with him, but I couldn't help it.

I'm not lying. I'm not holding stuff back . . . am I? The truth and the lies seem to mingle into a single story in my head when I'm stressed out.

What if Sam really did have a secret? I hadn't told anyone about that because I didn't know anything. Telling Mum and the police my brother had a secret but that I didn't think it really existed would just confuse matters.

And I'd apparently told Imran *I had something planned.*

What if somehow I'd managed to put Sam in danger?

And who could have been watching the house?

Had I been telling Imran the truth . . . or had I made it all up?

I just didn't know any more.

7

I manage to convince Jill everything is OK between me and Imran and she goes back to her discussions with Mum, Charlie and Augustine in the kitchen.

I sit in the chair with my eyes closed, taking deep breaths and willing myself to remember what I'd said to Imran at school on Friday. But it's like trying to see clearly through mud.

Ten minutes later, I hear commotion outside in the hallway. The front door opens and a blast of noise pours into the house again like a whoosh of thick black smoke.

The door thumps closed and cuts it out again, but there are some new gruff male voices in the hall.

I feel hot and a bit sick. It's probably the detectives come to speak to me again.

The living-room door opens and Jill comes in, followed by Mum and two men in ill-fitting navy suits. One is fat and bald, the other pencil thin with a shock of red hair that looks like a mop.

Charlie and Augustine both stand in the doorway, watching. Charlie's face is sour, but Augustine winks at me and I give her a weak smile.

'I'm Detective Inspector Fenton,' says the fatter man. 'And this is my colleague, Detective Sergeant Burnham.'

'Why aren't you in uniform?' I ask.

'Ed, honestly!' Mum rolls her eyes at the officers.

'It's a good question,' DI Fenton says. 'It's because we're CID, Ed; that's the Criminal Investigation Department. We're the detectives assigned to this very important case.'

'I shouted to him, but he wouldn't come,' I say in a rush. 'He was staring into the bushes, talking to himself.'

DI Fenton puts his hand up to silence me, and I press my lips together to seal in the panicky feeling that's suddenly seized me.

'Let's just start from the beginning, shall we?' the detective says calmly.

'Let's give Ed a little privacy,' Jill says, handing me a glass of water. 'Is it OK if I stay in here with you, Ed?'

I nod. 'I'd like Mum to stay too,' I say. But as soon as the words are out of my mouth, I could kick myself. I sound like a five-year-old wuss, wanting his mummy.

'Well . . . it might be better if the detectives talk to you on your own this time, Ed.' Jill glances at DI Fenton.

'And why's that, I wonder?' Charlie looks back from the doorway, his face thunderous. 'Gonna ask him if we're the ones who've kidnapped Sam, are you?'

'Charlie!' Mum cries out, and covers her mouth with a hand. 'Stop saying stuff like that.'

'Sorry I spoke,' he says sarcastically, and storms out of the room.

Augustine rolls her eyes at Mum and mouths an apology on Charlie's behalf.

'If Mrs Clayton would like to stay, that's fine.' DI Fenton smiles at Mum, but she stares at her hands as if she doesn't want to listen anyway.

'I don't mind sitting in, Lorraine,' Augustine says, touching her arm. 'If Ed doesn't mind, that is. You could go and get some rest.'

'Good idea, Augustine,' Jill says, and looks across at me. 'Is that OK with you, Ed?'

I nod and smile at Augustine. She's like a second mum to me, anyway.

DS Burnham gets out a small notepad and pen, and Mum shuffles out of the room.

'I was wondering, Ed,' DI Fenton says, 'if Bulwell Hall Park was somewhere that you and Sam went regularly? Even before yesterday, I mean.'

'We go there all the time.' I shrug. 'Sam really likes it there.'

'So let's go back a bit.' DI Fenton nods. 'Can you tell me about the time you both last went there . . . before yesterday. Can you remember when that was?'

I think for a moment. 'It was about a week ago. Sunday morning again – we go nearly every Sunday.'

'Fantastic.' He looks at DS Burnham, who scribbles

something down on his pad. 'So, Ed, tell me about that trip a week ago, especially what happened at the park. No matter how trivial it seems.'

'Forget we're here,' DS Burnham adds. 'Just say out loud exactly what you did there. Just the facts, please.'

A fleeting thought crosses my mind . . . Did he say that about only the facts because someone's told them I'm a liar? Because that's not fair.

Still, I nod and breathe a bit slower. I feel relieved I haven't got to go through everything that happened yesterday at the park again. Everything I can't remember.

Pictures of our trip to the park a week ago start to drift into my mind.

'We got to the park early afternoon, about two o'clock, I think. Sam wanted to find some sticklebacks, so I asked him where he wanted to pitch his spot.'

DS Burnham starts to make notes as I let the memories surface . . .

When we reached the bottom of the hill and it split off into two paths, Sam started running through the facts about Bulwell Hall. He'd always been fascinated by the now demolished building and we had a little routine every time we visited the park.

'Who built Bulwell Hall?' I started.

'John Newton in 1770.'

'When was it demolished?'

'1958.'

Sam rattled on about his favourite fact: how the Hall had been a camp for Italian prisoners of war when the British Army took it over at the start of World War Two.

I wasn't really listening by this time. My own stomach rumbles were distracting me and making me feel irritable.

'I want to go over there.' Sam pointed to our usual spot, near to the play park.

I glanced around. There was an old man with a stick walking his dog over the other side of the pond. A woman with a toddler and a pushchair walked towards the swings.

'That kid still has to use the baby swing,' Sam commented. 'He can't go on the big swings like me.'

'Hey, you were little once, you know.' I laughed at him, felt relaxed. It was a good time to be at the park. There was nobody around from school.

When we reached Sam's chosen fishing spot, I slipped off my rucksack and pulled out his glass jar. He took it from me and clambered to the edge of the water, scooping in the murky water.

I watched as he wobbled on the uneven bank. His wellies were at least two sizes too big. I'd found them in a skip outside one of the big three-storey houses on St Alban's Road. I'd brought them home for Sam, but then realized one of the heels had cracked right through. He'd refused to let me throw them away. But I knew if water got in while he fished, his socks and feet would get soaked and Mum would go mad.

'I think that's enough.' Sam held the water-filled jar up. His cheeks were flushed with happiness. 'It will keep the fish happy until they go back in.'

I sat on the side of the bank and took out my book, watching for a while as Sam scooped around in the water with his net. He crept along the edge of the water, plunging it in, dragging it across and pulling it out to inspect the contents.

I read Of Mice and Men for a bit, and then the sun came out and I put the book down and lay on my back, looking up at the sky.

I thought about how George and Lennie in the book left their home behind to start somewhere new. I thought about my home, all the things I didn't like, the things I wished I could change. Then I remembered the stuff that gave me a warm feeling in my belly, like listening to the rain pattering on the window outside when me and Sam were snuggled up in our beds, and last Christmas, when Mum had sold Grandma's gold and amethyst bracelet that she left her when she died. Augustine came over to help Mum cook dinner and we'd had presents and a proper turkey with pigs-in-blankets.

That was before Augustine met Charlie.

New places can be exciting but also scary because you don't know how things will turn out. When I'd first moved up from primary school to Bulwell Academy, a bit

43

of me felt excited, but mostly I had flutter belly and had to keep dashing to the loo.

I looked at the cover of my book and wondered if that's how George and Lennie felt, migrating to north California for a better life.

Augustine is staring at me. She's looking at me in a weird way, like she's just seeing me for the first time.

I stop talking, worried I've gone on a bit.

'You're doing great, Ed,' DI Fenton tells me. 'You're including loads of detail, which is just what we want.'

I take a sip of water and Augustine gives me a thumbs-up.

'So, you and Sam just sat there for a while. Sam was fishing; you were reading,' DS Burnham recaps, his pencil hovering above his notepad. 'How long would you say you sat like that?'

I thought for a moment. 'Probably about twenty minutes.'

'Good,' DS Burnham says, scribbling again. 'Please . . . carry on.'

Twenty minutes later, Sam had three small minnows zipping around his jar.

'I got the mum, the dad and the baby!' He held up the jar to the light. All the fish were the same size. He threw in a couple of leaves. 'These make it a nice home for them before they go back in the pond. Can you straighten up my net please, Ed?'

I pulled the wet and sagging net up by bending the wire and then I wiggled it on the end of the cane to make sure it was attached securely.

I heard Sam take a sharp breath in.

'Oh no.' His face was full of dread and he placed the jar down carefully in the long grass.

'What's wrong?' I followed his stare and then I saw why he was so upset.

Aidan Taylor and two of his mates were walking round the pond, heading straight for us.

8

'This boy . . . Aidan Taylor. Tell me about him,' DI Fenton says.

'He goes to my school.'

'Are you two mates?'

'No. I mean, we used to be, but . . .' I hesitate. 'We kind of just stopped being friends.'

Just after Dad got arrested, Aidan stopped asking me to play football after school with the others. I still played for the school team, though, for a while. Until the comments started in the changing rooms.

'Watch your valuables, lads,' Aidan joked. *'Lock everything up nice and safe.'*

'Yeah . . . there's the son of a criminal among us,' someone else muttered behind me.

Dad wasn't in prison because he'd stolen stuff or hurt anyone. He wasn't like that.

But I wasn't going to start explaining stuff to them when they'd already made their mind up about me.

I pushed my kit into my bag and walked out. And I never went back.

*

'Aidan Taylor is the same age as you, right?' DS Burnham asks.

I nod.

'And the other boys who were at the park, his mates . . . I'll need their names too, but for now, carry on. You're doing great, Ed.'

I thought the detectives would be firing angry questions at me, asking why I left Sam on his own yesterday, but they're not being like that at all.

We tried to ignore Aidan and the others, hoping they wouldn't see us, but of course they spotted us the second they got into the park.

'Who have we got here, then, lads? Oh look, it's liar, liar Edward Clayton and his little nose miner of a brother.'

'Don't call me that!' Sam yelled. 'I don't pick my nose.'

'Sorry, my mistake. You must be a mong instead, then.' Aidan stuck his tongue under his bottom lip. 'A stupid little mong of a nose miner.'

'Stop calling him that.' I stepped forward, pushing my fists in my pockets so they didn't see my hands shaking.

'Why, what you gonna do?' Aidan stepped closer to me. 'We're not in school now – you can't go crying to the teachers. He is a mong – why else would he have help with his reading and writing?'

They all burst out laughing, slapping Aidan on the back like he'd scored a goal or something.

I'd bitten down on my tongue. Our Sam went to a different school, and the only reason Aidan knew about his learning difficulties is because he used to be a friend I thought I could talk to.

'You never told me or your mum any of this, Ed!' Augustine sits on the edge of her chair and her eyes are moist. 'Why didn't you tell us you were being bullied?'

When *could* I have told Mum? She was always with Charlie or busy doing other stuff. If I tried to talk to her about anything at all, she just told me to stop whining. And Augustine does so much for us already that I didn't want to give her more problems to sort out.

Besides, I'd have felt like a little kid, telling tales.

Augustine looks at DI Fenton.

'This Aidan boy – is it possible him and his mates could've lured Sam away . . . is that why you want to know about him? I can't help thinking that you do sometimes hear about these things happening on the news.'

'Augustine,' Jill says gently. 'We can talk about this later, but for now please let Ed continue.'

DI Fenton nods to me and so I carry on.

'Stop saying that!' Sam had prodded at Aidan with his fishing net, holding it in front of him like a sword.

Justin Reed whipped round and snatched the cane

from Sam's hands. He held it high over his head, and Sam cowered as if he expected it to come crashing down on him.

'Hey! Leave him alone.' I lurched forward, tried to snatch it back, but Justin ran off to the side, and then I heard a loud crack.

'There you go, thicko.' He handed the net back to Sam in two pieces.

'Just go away and leave us alone.' Tears rolled down Sam's cheeks. 'You're just jealous cos you can't catch any fish like me.'

I saw him sneak a glance at his jar of fish in the grass.

I darted forward but it was too late. Bailey Marsh kicked the jar into the air like a football. Fish, pond water and leaves splodged everywhere.

'No!' Sam wailed. 'My fish family will die! They need to go back into the water.'

'They're just stupid, dumb fish.' Aidan laughed. 'If they're thick enough to get caught by you, they deserve to die. If you like water so much, why don't you go in the pond?'

'Leave him alone!' I shouted.

Aidan and I both dashed towards Sam at the same time. I don't think Aidan actually touched him – he just bluffed a shoving action. But in his panic, Sam stumbled backwards and toppled over into the water.

They all started laughing uncontrollably, but all I

could see was my brother, who couldn't swim, splashing around in the water.

I didn't know how deep the pond was, so I took off my fleece and waded in.

I managed to pull Sam back to the bank. He lay there, gasping like one of his fish.

Aidan, Justin and Bailey ran off to the park exit, laughing.

I helped Sam up to a sitting position.

'Come on, Sam. Don't let those idiots get to you,' I told him, but he was more worried about his fish.

'We have to find them, Ed, or they'll die.'

I didn't want to tell him they were probably already dead, so I pretended to find them in the grass and throw them back in.

'Were they all alive, Ed?' my brother asked me. 'Did you save them all?'

'Yes,' I told him. 'The mum, dad and baby, they're all swimming around together again. You can stop worrying now, Sam.'

I imagined the fish swimming around together and it felt so real in my mind.

9

'Time for a quick break, I think.' DI Fenton stands up and produces a packet of cigarettes from his inside jacket pocket. He turns to DS Burnham. 'Let's have five minutes in the back garden, Josh.'

'You did really well there, love,' Augustine whispers to me as she follows Jill into the other room.

A few seconds later, I'm sitting there alone.

I hope I'm not going to get in trouble with Mum. The account I've just given the detectives is a lot different to the one I gave at home when I eventually got Sam back from the park.

Mum, Augustine and Charlie were in the kitchen that day when we finally got back to Grindon Crescent.

'Oh, you're wet through, love,' Mum cried out, and hugged Sam to her. 'What happened?'

Sam hesitated, looked at me.

'Well? You heard your mother.' Charlie scowled. 'You were supposed to be looking after your brother. So, how come he's soaked to the skin, but you're absolutely fine?'

I wanted to tell him to get lost. Since Dad went to

51

prison, Charlie seemed to think it was up to him to step into his shoes, when our lives have nothing to do with him.

'He means well, Ed,' Mum had said once when I told her it bugged me. 'He just doesn't want you going off the rails while your dad is inside.'

Yeah, right. More like he hates me and uses any excuse to have a go.

Mum turned back to Sam. 'Something bad happened at the park, didn't it?'

Sam didn't answer. He just stared at me, like Mum, Augustine and Charlie were doing too. The cogs in my head began to whir like crazy.

'We went down to the park because Sam was hungry and there was nothing in for breakfast,' I said all in one breath.

'Get on with it and leave out the bleeding-heart story,' Charlie snapped.

Augustine nudged him. 'Go easy on the lad, then.'

'We went to Bulwell Hall Park and Sam wanted to do some fishing with his net and jar. That's right, isn't it, Sam?'

'Yes,' Sam mumbled as Mum pulled him closer.

'And that's when the terrible thing happened.'

'Which was?' Charlie bellowed. 'Christ, if you were writing a book it'd be twice as thick as any other. Get on with it.'

'Charlie!' Augustine looked at me. 'What happened at the park, love?'

I didn't want Mum to know I'd been scared of Aidan Taylor and the others.

I wanted her to be proud.

'Sam started fishing when the sky darkened and it all went quiet. The birds stopped singing and the cows all lay down in the field, like when there's an eclipse.'

'What field?' Charlie smirked. 'I haven't seen any cows or any field down Bulwell Hall Park lately.'

I could see the cows and the field in my head. I could see our Sam shaking and afraid. In my imagination, I took charge of the situation.

'The pond water started bubbling, like it was being boiled. I shouted to Sam to get out of the water, but he didn't hear me cos of the noise and—'

'I thought you said it all went quiet?' Mum had pressed her lips together in a straight line. She always does that when she doesn't believe me.

'And then the water exploded!' I made an impressive exploding noise and let my arms and fingers fly out for extra effect. 'And out came this thing . . . this monster.'

'Was it the Loch Ness Monster? Maybe he's down here on his holidays,' Charlie said, his voice dripping with sarcasm.

'No, it'd be the Bulwell Hall Monster,' Mum added, but she didn't laugh. She just shook her head sadly at me.

'It wasn't a monster exactly. It was . . . it was a giant carp.'

I just couldn't seem to stop.

'It was the biggest fish I've ever seen, even bigger than those on telly or in one of Dad's fishing magazines, and its mouth was hanging wide open, heading straight for our Sam.'

I paused for a moment to get my breath and they all stared at me . . . Mum, Augustine, Charlie and even Sam.

'I snatched Sam out of the water and carried him up the bank to safety. Everyone started clapping and someone took a photo. They said it might be in the local paper next week.'

Mum blinked steadily at me. Charlie shook his head. Sam and Augustine stayed quiet.

'But then the carp still kept coming and—'

Mum raised her hand in a stop sign. Her face looked droopy and pale like dough.

'Sam,' she said softly, putting her finger under my brother's chin and tilting it, so he looked directly up at her. 'Tell me, how did you get so wet today?'

Sam and I looked at each other. I knew he didn't want to show me up as a liar, but he didn't really have a choice.

'Aidan Taylor and two other boys pushed me in the pond,' he said.

Why couldn't I just have said that?

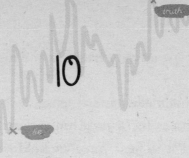

10

The crowd outside the gate have moved to one side.

There's a battered old camper van now parked outside our house. Next to it, a large white removal lorry has its back doors wide open and I can see it's full of furniture. It looks like someone is moving into one of the converted flats next door.

As I stare at the camper van, one of the net curtains twitches and I'm sure I see someone moving behind it. I stand there a bit longer, waiting to see if a face appears from behind the grubby patterned lace hanging at the windows. But nobody does.

There are a lot of new people on the street that we don't know now. Mum has one or two friends around here, but that's all.

People seemed to fade away when Dad went to prison.

'Best to keep ourselves to ourselves,' Mum had said when one or two people crossed the road rather than speak to her. 'Why give folks a chance to look down their nose at us?'

Without Dad's wages coming in, things got really tight at home. Mum tried to get another cleaning job on top of the two she already had, but she just couldn't manage it.

Augustine made her see sense.

'You can't fix everything, Lorraine,' she'd said. 'Sometimes you just have to hold your hands up and accept the worst has happened. Anyone judging you so quickly without knowing the facts isn't worth knowing. If you carry on trying to be everything to everybody, you'll make yourself very ill.'

Mum and Augustine made a bit of a deal. She'd cut back on hours, and Augustine would help out as much as she could.

She started topping up the electricity meter, bringing cooked meals round for me, and even let us have a bath or shower round hers when there was no hot water.

We missed Dad terribly, but after a while Sam stopped crying himself to sleep and, although things weren't the same as before, Augustine helped us all to feel that it wasn't so bad.

Then she met Charlie and everything changed.

Augustine pops her head round the door. 'Want a glass of pop, love?'

I nod and she steps inside and pushes the door closed behind her.

'I know it's hard, thinking back over stuff you and Sam

did together, but it'll help find him. You know that, don't you?'

I nod.

'What's wrong, Ed? Since your friend Imran left, you seem really low.'

It's because I can't get what Imran said out of my head. The stuff about someone watching the house.

'You can tell me anything, you know.' Augustine walks over and sits next to me.

I just want to get the worry that I did something wrong out of my head, let someone else deal with it. Would it really do any harm to confide in Augustine?

'Imran said I'd told him something. Before Sam went missing . . . But the thing is, I can't remember saying anything at all. If I keep saying that to the police, they're going to get annoyed because I can obviously remember *some* things.'

'What exactly did you tell him?' Augustine whispers as we hear the kitchen door open and close.

'He said I'd told him that—'

The detectives' voices are outside the door.

'Look, if you feel uncomfortable, then say nothing about it now,' Augustine says in a low voice. 'You can tell me when the detectives have gone and then we can discuss whether to get them back in. That means less pressure on you.'

'Thanks.' I smile, feeling relieved. Talking to Augustine

about what I supposedly told Imran might even jog my memory. I'll feel more relaxed with her than with the police.

The two detectives walk back in. DI Fenton heaves himself into the chair again.

'Let's carry on where we left off, then. Back to the park a week last Sunday—'

'Can I just ask,' Augustine interrupts. 'Why are you focusing on their visit to the park last week, when Sam actually went missing yesterday?'

It's a good question. I was thinking the same myself, even though I feel relieved we're talking around the terrible event itself.

'Certainly. Ed is having difficulty recalling the whole incident when Sam went missing,' DI Fenton explains. 'By starting with events he *can* remember, we're hoping some blocked memories may be recalled.'

'Blocked memories about *what* exactly?' Augustine presses him.

DI Fenton glances at me and coughs.

'Well, if the park was a place the boys visited regularly, it's feasible that a potential abductor could have tracked their movements . . . Perhaps Ed noticed something unusual at the time, but for the moment it's escaped him.'

Had there been someone watching me and Sam? The same person who had been watching the house?

I can feel the dreadful weight of what happened, but for some reason, I can't reach it.

'I understand.' Augustine nods.

'So, Ed.' DS Burnham turns to me again. 'That day, after Aidan and his mates left the park, what did you and Sam do? Did you go straight home?'

I had persuaded Sam to go to our den rather than go straight back home.

'You don't want Mum to see you in that state, do you?' I asked Sam.

'I'm really hungry, though,' he grumbled. 'And very wet.'

'We'll only stay a bit,' I told him. 'You get to be the king of the den. OK?'

I feel bad cos I was really just trying to save my own skin. I thought that if we waited in the den a while, Mum might be out when we got back.

Sometimes Mum seemed to barely notice we'd been gone at all. Other times she'd be waiting, angry and upset, ready to tell us off for just disappearing. We were never sure which version of Mum we'd get.

I helped Sam up, dusted off the leaves and all the grass that was stuck to him, and we headed back across the park, towards the hill.

'What if Aidan is still hanging around up at the top?' He twisted his fingers together in front of him.

'He won't be,' I said confidently, but it was just to cover up my nervousness. I thought that Aidan and his gang would probably already be searching for their next victim.

We walked around the pond and past the play park. I held my breath as we turned left and started climbing the hill. There was a clear view right up to the top and I was relieved when I saw there was nobody up there, especially Aidan and his dumb mates.

'When will Dad be out of prison?' Sam asked me suddenly. It was weird because we hadn't been talking about him.

'Maybe in a few weeks,' I said. 'There's been a hearing and they're starting to believe that Dad is innocent. So . . . they might let him out and he'd be home with us by Christmas. If he is, we can show him our den and he can—'

'Ed, I know that's not true.' Sam threw me a sideways glance. 'Dad isn't going to be out for Christmas, is he?'

'Well, maybe not exactly Christmas, but soon. It could be very soon.'

Augustine sits bolt upright in her seat and I stop talking to look at her.

'Where have you heard that, Ed?' she asks sharply. 'Your dad's got a new release date?'

'Please, let's just let Ed finish.' DI Fenton sounds irritated.

'Sorry.' Augustine sits back and folds her arms.

'I don't know why I said that stuff to Sam,' I say, hanging my head. 'I wanted to make him feel better. And me too.'

'That's OK, Ed.' Jill nods. 'Just carry on.'

'My teacher talked to me about Dad,' Sam snapped. 'She told me Dad's not going to be out for a very long time.'

'What does she know?' I kicked bits of bracken back from the path as I walked. 'She's got no flipping right telling you that—'

'Mum was there too,' Sam said. 'They both said it was better for me to know the truth than to keep hoping Dad might come home soon.'

'How come nobody's told me *that?' I felt a column of heat channelling up towards my head like a hot wire. 'How come nobody ever tells me anything?'*

'But Mum did tell us.' Sam rolled his eyes. 'When Dad first got banged up.'

'Yeah, but . . . Mum just said he'd got fifteen years. She didn't bother sitting down with my teacher, did she?' I knew I was being mardy, but I couldn't help it.

Sam didn't reply and we walked up the hill in silence. The only sound was birdsong and our feet scuffing the loose pebbles and sending them firing out at all angles.

I knew we were both thinking the same thing: Dad being in prison sucked.

'Why did you say it, Ed?' Sam stopped walking and looked at me.

'Huh?'

'All that stuff . . . lies. About Dad being home for Christmas?'

'It wasn't exactly lies. I was just—'

'It is lies! You're always telling lies.' He glared at me and I saw his eyes were dark and shining with tears. 'Dad's not coming back.'

'It could happen,' I still argued. 'If Dad was proved innocent, they'd let him out right away.'

'If all the prisoners were proved innocent, they'd all be out for Christmas.' A solitary tear snaked down my brother's dirty cheek, leaving a clean trail. 'But they're not. They're not innocent and they won't be let out.'

'I wasn't lying.' I tried to reason with him. 'I was just saying there's a possibility he might be out soon, that's all.'

Sam sniffed, but he didn't answer. He was upset and shivering. I wanted to hug him, but, the mood he was in, he probably would have thumped me.

When we got up to Barker's Wood, I checked around to make sure nobody was watching. The last thing we wanted was for Aidan and his goons to follow us in and smash up our den.

It was darker in there, the ground damp and marshy under the shade of the trees. We walked down the main path and then, just before the big tree stump, we veered off left, making sure we arranged the branches and bushes behind us so there was no obvious gap left.

I felt something brush against my fingers and realized it was Sam, reaching across to hold my hand. Usually I'd call him a wuss, but I could understand it that day – it was pretty creepy in there.

A branch cracked somewhere deeper in the wood and we both froze. I pressed my finger to my lips and we both fell silent. Someone whooped and then there was loud laughter.

We looked at each other, both recognizing the voice with dread.

'It's Aidan,' Sam whispered, fear in his eyes.

'Come on,' I hissed. 'We're nearly at the den.'

Creeping on the balls of our feet, we slipped through the trees. We could clearly hear Aidan and the others and, although I didn't say anything to Sam, their laughter was definitely getting closer. My heart pumped faster and my breathing felt shallow and rushed, but I just kept on moving in the direction of the den, making sure Sam was close behind me.

A few seconds later, we stopped walking.

To anyone else, we were standing in the middle of a tangle of tree branches and brambles, but that wasn't the case. We'd stumbled upon it by accident a few months *earlier. Sam tripped and fell through what we thought were bushes, but it led to this little clearing.*

We'd worked on it since then. Strengthened the camouflage at the entrance and done some clearing and organizing inside. It was our place, somewhere only we knew about.

Sam slipped past me and appeared to walk straight into a wall of branches and leaves, but, when he reached it, the heavy curtain of foliage parted and suddenly he disappeared.

As the voices drew closer, I slipped through the leaves too, and we crouched there, hardly daring to breathe.

The detectives look at each other meaningfully, and then DS Burnham starts writing furiously.

'Can you take us there, Ed?' DI Fenton says quickly. 'To the den? That's if you feel up to it.'

I nod. 'Course.'

'Are you thinking Sam might be hiding there?' Augustine gasps.

I feel a prickle on the back of my neck.

Why didn't I think of that?

12

DI Fenton steps outside the room and I hear him make a call. I can't catch everything he says, but the gist of it is that more officers will be coming and we'll be taking a trip out to our den.

I feel a bit unsettled inside. Sam and I had always agreed – had made a cast-iron promise – that we'd never tell anyone else about our den.

But sometimes you have to decide if a promise is worth breaking.

Sam might've run off at the park, but gone back to our den later on. He would be cold and hungry and in danger there.

That's when I know for sure I'm doing the right thing for my brother in taking the police to our secret den. The blipping in my chest eases.

'I didn't know you two boys had a den, Ed.' Augustine grins. 'Little dark horse, aren't you?'

I grin back at her. Mum would've probably told me off for having a secret, but Augustine is always cool about stuff like that.

DI Fenton reappears in the room and sits back down.

'We've checked your mum is happy for you to go to the den, Ed, and she says it's fine if you're feeling OK.'

'I don't feel unwell at all and I want to help find my brother.'

'Great. Well, while we're waiting for the car, do you want to just finish telling us what happened in the wood that day, Ed?'

The voices of Aidan and the others got closer and closer.

'I saw the rabbit run this way.' I recognized Bailey Marsh's voice. 'Maybe we can corner it.'

'Yeah, like proper hunters,' Aidan added.

Sam's eyes widened and I rolled my eyes at him as if they were just bluffing. But really it made me feel sick to hear them excited about chasing a poor defenceless rabbit.

I thought about Aidan's cruel comment about Sam's fish deserving to die and wondered what makes them want to hurt every living thing they set eyes on.

Closer and closer, their voices came.

Sam never took his eyes off my face, and I had to try really hard to keep my expression neutral. My back felt wet with sweat, and my hands were damp and clammy.

What if one of them stumbled against the leaves like Sam did? That's how we'd found the den in the first place.

If they walked really close to the den entrance and hit out at the branches and leaves with their sticks . . . the 'wall' might move and they'd realize it was actually an entrance.

I tried to slow down my breathing, to take in a bit more air, but it was difficult. Even in the gloom of all the thick leaves and branches around us, I could see Sam's face had drained of colour and he'd stopped watching me. His eyes were now squeezed tightly shut as if he'd taken himself to another place altogether.

They were almost on top of us now. We heard sticks smashing into tree trunks, heavy feet trampling on bracken, and rough hands snapping young saplings.

Sam grabbed hold of my sleeve. I could feel him trembling.

I braced myself to jump at whoever was first through the den entrance. I planned to push Sam back and keep their attention on me.

Somehow, my fear had disappeared and I'd found myself in a place where I just thought about protecting my brother.

'Arrgghhh!' One of them emitted a loud war cry, and then Aidan yelled, 'There's the prey – that way!'

We heard scuffling, laughter, breathlessness . . . and then silence. They were gone, probably heading for Aidan's house on nearby Golf Close.

Sam opened his eyes and I let out the breath I seemed to have been holding for ages.

'Are they going to kill that rabbit?' Sam asked tearfully.

'Nah, they're far too dumb, Sam.' I grinned at him. 'Rabbits are smart creatures. It'll be having fun getting those idiots running around the woods all day.'

His frown disappeared. 'Yeah, rabbits are really fast runners. They'll never manage to catch it.'

Then he asked me, 'Are you scared of Aidan Hunt? Or of Justin, and Bailey?'

'Are you joking?'

He looked steadily back at me, but he didn't say anything.

'No! I'm not scared of them.' I puffed out my chest a bit. 'I just don't cause trouble when you're with me cos you're little and—'

'I'm not little – I'm eight!'

'Well, anyway, that's why I didn't say much to them at the park, but if we'd have been at school it'd be a different story, I can tell you that.'

'Like how?'

'I'd have drop-kicked them to the ground, one by one.'

Sam laughed.

'What? You don't believe me? I was trying to keep this a secret, but I suppose it won't hurt to tell you. I've been taking kung fu lessons . . . in secret.'

'Where?'

'At a community centre near here. You don't know it.'

'Liar!'

I bit down hard on my tongue and a metallic taste filled my mouth. 'Don't call me a liar.'

'So . . . where'd you get the money for the classes, then?'

Sam looked as if he was trying hard not to laugh. Sometimes, I'd seen other people look like that when I started telling stories.

'The classes are free.'

'Can I go?'

'No! You're too young. Also, the instructor says I've got a natural talent for it. They reckon I could be a champion if I want to enter the competition circuit.'

'A champion? What about last year when you were in Year Seven and practising kung fu kicks on the school field and you slipped and twisted your ankle? Dad had to come and get you and take you to the walk-in centre to see a doctor.'

'Yeah, but I wasn't doing it right then, was I? I'm getting some proper training in now with professionals. I could take Aidan out any time I want to. I could drop-kick all of them to the floor.'

I pictured myself in the proper martial arts uniform, accepting the winner's trophy in a top competition.

I liked this version of me much more than the one whose hands shook when Aidan Taylor came looking for trouble.

'Yeah, yeah, yeah.' Sam yawned.

Sam asked Mum later if it was true, and she rolled her eyes at Augustine and Charlie.

'He's a liar, just like his old man,' Charlie said smoothly. He never missed a chance to put Dad down. 'Kung fu expert? It's the funniest thing I ever heard.' He grinned at me. 'You couldn't fight your way out of a paper bag.'

Every now and again the breeze carried Aidan and co's voices back, faint in the distance.

I stood up and pulled my T-shirt away from the stickiness on my back, stretching up to touch the bent branches above my head.

Sam had already started picking up fallen leaves from the floor. We came a few times a week and did some clearing work to keep it tidy. Mum moaned that our bedroom was always a mess. Sometimes I wished we could show her our den, how neat we kept it, but it would probably just make her angry.

Walking home from school one day, I'd spotted a ground sheet stuffed in a wheelie bin, the sort painters and decorators use to keep paint splatters off the carpet. It had made a brilliant carpet for the packed-down earth floor in our den.

Mrs Lahore down our road threw out two stripy deckchairs and a red tartan wool blanket. They were folded up and leaning on the gate waiting for the dustbin men. She saw me and our Sam looking.

'You want them, boys? Then take them. But one of

them is torn, and the picnic blanket has a scorch mark from when Mr Lahore put it too close to the fire pit.'

'Thanks, Mrs Lahore,' I said as Sam and I took a chair each. 'These will be brilliant for our . . . garden. Me and my dad like to sit out with the telescope and watch the planets at night.'

She gave me this little smile and shook her head. Watched us as we walked off with the deckchairs.

'You could've just said we wanted them for our den,' Sam grumbled as we walked. 'You didn't have to say all that stuff about watching planets with Dad when really he's in prison.'

'She won't know about that.' I shrugged, still imagining how cool it would be to sit out with Dad and look at the planets.

'Yes she will.' Sam scowled at me. 'Everybody round here knows Dad's in prison. Your stories don't make any difference.'

'Yes they do,' I snapped back. 'They're much better than the scabby truth.'

13

'Right. Let's leave it there for now,' DI Fenton says. 'Our car will be here very soon and then you can show us your secret den.'

Maybe he's hoping Sam has run away of his own accord and is hiding in our den. Deep down I know how scared Sam gets when he's alone in the dark. I don't think he'd have gone there without me. But the thought he could be back sleeping in our bedroom tonight makes me hope against all odds.

A text comes through on DI Fenton's phone. He reads it and frowns, showing it to DS Burnham. They both stand up.

'Back in five,' DI Fenton tells Augustine, and they walk out into the hallway.

Mum and Charlie come into the living room. Mum sits next to Augustine, and Charlie stands at the window. He moves the blind a bit and the crowd at the gate surges forward. The photographers hold up cameras with enormous zoom lenses. Charlie has his back to the room, but I can see his face from the side. He smiles really faintly to himself.

'I'd come away from the window if I were you, Charlie,'

Augustine says curtly. 'You don't want to attract those jackals any more than we have already.'

Charlie glares at her, but says nothing and steps away from the window. He never speaks to Augustine horribly, like he does the rest of us. She'd snap his head off if he did. I'm glad she's here.

'So, did you remember anything more about Sam going missing?' Charlie turns from the window and scowls at me.

I ignore him and look at Mum. 'They want me to show them our den.'

'Den? What den's that?' Mum asks.

'Ed did really well, telling the police about when he and Sam hid from bullies in their secret den,' Augustine tells Mum. 'It's in the woods, near Bulwell Hall Park.'

'Close to where Sam went missing?' Charlie says. 'Why didn't you mention this before, Einstein?'

'I—'

'Don't tell me.' Charlie rolls his eyes. '*You forgot.*'

'I just didn't think to mention it,' I say, feeling stupid.

Mum starts to cry softly and my heart feels like it's splitting in two.

If only I could remember what I'd told Imran. Who could have been watching the house? This could be a good time to tell Mum.

I shift in my seat and lock my fingers together. 'There's something I—'

'Have you remembered something?' Mum pleads.

'Let's not push Ed too hard,' Augustine says, looking at me meaningfully.

I remember she said I could discuss what Imran said with her and she'd help me decide if it was useful. I don't want to get Mum's hopes up or the police to get annoyed because I can't give them any details.

'I'm sure he'll remember things very soon. He needs a bit of space to think,' she adds, smiling at me.

I press my lips together in a tiny smile to show Augustine I'm grateful for her calming Mum down.

'I'm not sure yet, but I think I'll remember soon. I can feel I'm close to it,' I tell Mum.

'I knew you'd seen something you weren't telling us or the police,' Charlie says accusingly. 'Aside from talking to bushes and all that baloney.'

I freeze for a moment as an image flits through my mind. Sam's face, trees, and then something else, maybe a shadow . . . or a person? I reach for it, but it's already gone.

'What is it, Ed?' Mum sits bolt upright, watching my face.

'Nothing.' I sigh.

'Told you, Lorraine.' Charlie turns back to the window. 'He's a little liar through and through and we'll never get the truth out of him.'

14

The noise level outside is on the rise again. I stand up and move close to the window, but I don't touch the blind.

The sprawling crowd of people is still outside the front gate. Our neighbours look worried, but the other people, the reporters and photographers, they're standing around in little groups, talking to each other.

My eye is drawn to the camper van next door. A girl stands, leaning back on it with her arms crossed. She stares straight at the house. She can't possibly see me here, but her eyes are focused on the window like she can.

I wonder if she's moved in next door.

The journalists and TV people are tapping away on their phones and tablets and showing each other stuff on the screens. Their bored expressions have evaporated and suddenly they're buzzing like bees.

The door of the kitchen is pulled to but not closed. I hover around outside for a few seconds and hear Mum say, 'Isn't there anything we can do to stop them?'

I push the door open and see they're all looking at DI Fenton's phone. Everyone closes their mouths and stares at me.

'You OK there, Ed?' Charlie says. He's acting all nice in

front of the police, but he doesn't fool me.

I look at Mum, at Jill and Augustine. They don't meet my eyes.

'What's wrong?' I ask.

'Nothing! Nothing's wrong, love. The detectives are just keeping us informed of what's happening behind the scenes,' Augustine says quickly.

DI Fenton slides his phone in his pocket and coughs.

Mum is staring into space, flicking her thumb and finger together really fast like she does when she's worried about paying the rent.

'Will somebody just tell me what's happened?' I say.

Even in here, I can hear that the crowd outside is getting noisier. Something is wrong.

Mum suddenly turns to Jill.

'Tell him,' she whispers hoarsely.

'Ed, the detectives came to tell us that the press have been digging into things, as they unfortunately always do, in these cases,' Jill says. 'Sadly, instead of focusing on what's happened to Sam, it's taking the positive publicity we need off on a tangent, so we need to deal with it sensitively.'

She's talking in riddles.

'So . . . what's happened?' I ask, looking at them all in turn.

DI Fenton slides his phone out of his pocket and steps forward. 'I'm afraid the press have found out your dad is in prison, Ed.' He taps at the screen and holds it up so I can see. 'The information hasn't come from us – they just have underhand ways of finding this stuff out.'

It's a tweet and it includes a link to a news website. I take the phone and click on the link, turning my back to them to read the article.

Monday, 23 July

FATHER OF MISSING LOCAL BOY IS CONVICTED CRIMINAL

It has emerged that the father of missing 8-year-old local boy Samuel Clayton is serving the third year of his ten-year sentence and is detained at Category B prison HMP Nottingham.

A neighbour, who wished to remain anonymous, said that it had been a shock when Mr Clayton was tried and convicted of fraud two years ago.

'Most folks around here are law-abiding,' the 40-year-old man said. 'We didn't know much about it because the family is quite secretive. They never talk about Phil being a convicted criminal, but we all know about it. The family is not well-liked.'

The boy, known to friends and family as Sam, went missing late on Sunday afternoon while visiting Bulwell Hall Park with his 14-year-old brother, Edward.

The children were out alone at the time.

Another neighbour said, 'We see the boys out and about on their own quite frequently. Sometimes, they can't get in their house after school. On occasion, I've had to give them a snack and a drink.'

Due to an accident involving Sam's brother falling from play equipment and sustaining a head injury, police say it is still not clear exactly how Sam went missing, nor what happened in the minutes leading up to his disappearance.

Over 200 volunteers took part in a three-hour fingertip search of the park and nearby woodland.

Police are asking witnesses to come forward. They would still like to question a bearded man of dishevelled appearance with light-brown short hair who was seen in the area shortly before Sam's disappearance. He wore a blue checked shirt and beige trousers tucked into tan-coloured boots.

Door-to-door enquiries and a wider search are taking place, and police say they are still working on leads.

Anyone who saw Sam at the park or who has any further information, can contact Nottinghamshire Police confidentially.

15

The article has already been retweeted 565 times. I hand the detective back his phone.

'You shouldn't have asked neighbours for food and drink after school,' Mum says tearfully. 'I didn't know you were doing that.'

'I didn't! It only happened once. Mrs Lahore gave us a drink and a biscuit each. We didn't ask for it.'

'Might have known that interfering old bag would have something to say about us,' Charlie growled.

'OK, let's try to keep things cool,' Jill says.

'So, what about my son?' Mum turns on Jill, a deep pink bloom flooding her cheeks. 'All this messing about, gossiping that Phil is in prison, arguing about which neighbour gave my boys a snack . . . What about our Sam? What are you doing to find him?'

Jill takes a breath, ready to tackle Mum's fury. 'Lorraine, I know it's difficult, but you have to trust us to—'

'*Trust you?*' Mum's eyes brim over. 'You seem more interested in following Twitter gossip than focusing on the case. Shouldn't you should be out there, finding out what happened to Sam?'

DI Fenton coughs.

Jill hands her a tissue, but Mum ignores it and wipes her eyes with her sleeve.

'There are about a hundred officers out there as we speak, knocking on doors, speaking to locals. And we're drafting in more officers from neighbouring forces.'

'What good is that going to do?' Charlie chips in. *'Talking to people?* We need an arrest!'

'We still don't know exactly what has happened to Sam,' Jill says gently, still looking at Mum.

'Well, you're not going to find out sat in here drinking tea, are you?' Charlie snipes.

Jill pauses. 'We have to rule out certain things, right at the beginning of the investigation . . . It's just something that has to be done, unfortunately.'

Mum sniffs and looks at her. 'What things?'

Charlie stands up, his arms rigid. 'Oh, I get it. You're trying to find out if we've got anything to do with Sam going missing, yes? We're your major suspects right now . . . Sam's own family.'

'Sit down and shut up, Charlie,' Augustine says, looking at Mum.

Mum's mouth falls open. 'Is that true?'

'No!' Jill glares at Charlie and then her face softens when she speaks to Mum again. 'It's not true, Lorraine. Nobody is a formal suspect here, but we have to look at all sorts of things and rule them out. I'm afraid that's the nature of a serious investigation.'

'What sorts of things?' Mum narrows her eyes. Her voice sounds sharp and annoyed, but I know her too well. Just under the surface, I can see that she's ready to fall apart.

'Mrs Clayton,' DS Burnham speaks up. 'Is it true that Sam has run away from home before?'

A cloak of silence falls on the room and Mum's hands start to shake.

It *is* true.

Sam has run off twice before.

16

The first time, Sam ran off because Charlie – who had no right – confiscated his toy cars for treading mud through Augustine's house. The second time, it was because he hadn't learned his spellings and he was scared of going to school the next day and doing the test.

'It's not true.' Mum's voice is dangerously high. 'He's never run away from home. Not properly, anyhow.'

'Not properly, you say, but he *has* run off before . . . in a fashion?' DI Fenton presses her.

'Only in one of his tantrums. Just silly things.' The colour drains from Mum's face. 'And never for very long. He came back within an hour or two.'

DS Burnham stops writing. 'When did this happen, Sam running away?'

'It's happened twice in the last year,' Mum says. 'But it wasn't the same as this, at all. He's never gone *seriously* missing, like now.'

The detectives look at each other.

'I'm sick to death of this. I'm going out there to look for him myself,' Mum says, standing up. 'I can't just sit here when nothing is being done. Where is he? What if somebody's hurting him? What if . . . ?'

Mum begins to whimper. She covers her head with her arms and curls inward, making herself into a ball shape. Augustine moves closer to her and gently strokes her back.

All I had to do was watch my brother yesterday and all this could have been avoided. Today would have just been a normal day and Mum would've been OK.

'Lorraine, please. I know it's unbearable, but you must stick with us on this.' Jill looks meaningfully at the two detectives.

Charlie scowls. 'Surprise, surprise. More sitting around doing nothing.'

Jill shakes her head.

'There's lots being done, Charlie, but, as I've explained, we have to be methodical in ticking off the boxes. It would be disastrous to miss anything that's relevant at this stage.'

Charlie rolls his eyes.

'Lorraine is the only person here entitled to ask questions about the way we conduct this investigation.' Jill looks as if she's had enough of his sarcasm. '*She* is Sam's parent.'

'Nice. In other words, *keep your nose out*,' Charlie snaps at her.

'I'm saying please try not to constantly interfere, Charlie. It's not helpful.'

'Somebody's got to look out for Lorraine, haven't they? Make sure you lot are pulling your weight.'

Jill's nostrils flare and she glances at DI Burnham and they leave the room.

Charlie peers out past the blind again, pulling it up further than before.

The press start shouting and beckoning for him to go out there.

'They'll never leave us alone now,' Mum says. 'They'll just keep digging up more stuff about what a bad mother I am.'

Charlie stands up a little straighter, but he keeps his voice low so only we can hear. 'Leave it to me, Lorraine. I'll talk to them, love. Someone's got to give them your side of the story.'

'I don't think we should say anything to the newspapers,' Mum says quickly. 'Jill said it's best to ignore them.'

Charlie bangs the windowsill with the flat of his hand.

'They're trashing you, though, saying anything they like with no comeback. Is that what you want?'

Mum stays quiet.

'These big newspapers, they pay good money for the inside story.' Charlie looks out of the window and licks his lips. 'It could be the answer to all your problems.'

'But the police have said we shouldn't—'

'What do the police know? They've been messing about all this time when they could've been out there, looking for Sam.' Charlie scowls again. 'They'll never find him at this rate. Everybody knows the first forty-eight hours are vital.'

'Don't!' Mum cries out. 'Don't keep saying that. I can't bear it.'

Charlie rounds on me and snarls, pointing at the wall clock. 'What time is it?'

'Ten past four,' I mutter, wondering what he's getting at.

'See, he can remember how to tell the time, Lorraine. If he'd *really* lost his memory, he wouldn't remember anything at all, would he?'

'I think that's a different sort of memory.' Mum's voice sounds shaky and a bit weird. 'The doctors said he'll be OK remembering tasks and stuff, but he has a block about what happened at the park.'

'How convenient.'

I feel Charlie's eyes burning into me, but I don't look at him.

17

Jill appears in the doorway.

'Car's here, Ed. You ready?'

I nod and stand up.

'I'll come with ya,' Charlie snaps. 'I want to see this bloody den you've been keeping from your mum, giving Sam ideas to hide out there.'

'I don't think that's a very good idea, under the circumstances, sir,' DI Fenton says firmly.

'His mother ought to go, then,' Charlie insists. 'Or Augustine.'

Mum doesn't comment. She's squashed into the corner of the settee like she's trying to shrink down under the seat cushions.

'It's probably best if Ed shows us himself,' DI Fenton says carefully. 'Without you or Mrs Clayton this time.'

'Why's that, then?' Charlie balls his fists. 'I know why – it's cos you think *we've* got summat to do with Sam going missing.'

'No, that's not the case. But we've already explained the procedure for serious crime investigations, sir,' DI Fenton says calmly. 'Once we've ticked all the boxes, we can move on.'

Jill looks at me. 'Is there anyone else you'd like with you, Ed?'

'I can go with him . . . if Ed wants me to, that is.' Augustine walks over to Mum and sits down next to her. 'You get some rest, Lorraine. You know I'll look after him.'

'Thanks,' Mum whispers.

'I'll stay here and look after your mum, Ed,' Jill says.

Nobody mentions Charlie. Nobody looks at him when he sits down heavily in the chair and starts drumming his stumpy fingers on his knees.

We wait in the hallway. Me, Augustine and the two detectives.

'When the officers open the door, just keep your head down and let them lead you to the car, Ed,' DS Burnham tells me. 'Don't speak to anyone. Don't answer any questions.'

I nod. My throat feels dry, too dry to swallow, and my ears are burning. When I touch them, they feel red hot.

Questions hit my ears like little sharp arrows as soon as we step outside.

'Has anyone been to prison to tell Phil Clayton his son is missing?'

'Has the family friend, Charlie, got an alibi?'

'Did you see anyone take your brother, Ed?'

I don't speak, don't look around. I don't want to see any more banners blaming Mum. I keep my eyes on the path.

When we get out of the gate, the officers move close in front and behind me. The crowd surges forward and jostles us.

'Stay back!' one of the officers demands. 'Move back. Now!'

I feel a firm hand on the top of my head and I duck down and climb in the back of the big police van, Augustine sitting next to me.

Only when the vehicle pulls away do I allow myself to glance out of the window.

The girl I saw by the camper van has turned round and is watching me intently.

Twenty minutes later, we pull up at the top end of the park by the woods.

There are press cars and vans following, but the police have set up a cordon and closed the park, so they can't follow us all the way up there.

I get out of the van and I hear a blackbird singing nearby. Sam always loved listening to the birds when we were here. He could identify every one by its whistle.

A lump lodges in my throat. I try to swallow it down, but it won't shift.

'Lead the way, Ed,' DI Fenton tells me, and off we go. There are about ten police officers with us now and there's an ambulance parked up too.

Augustine notices my shaking hands and she grasps my fingers as we walk, holding on to them in her own warm hand.

'You're doing bloody brilliant,' she whispers. 'D'ya hear me?'

I nod.

'Soon be over,' she says. 'He'll be home soon. I know it.'

But she can't know that, not really. She can only hope like the rest of us.

I imagine getting to the den and parting the leaf curtain and there's Sam, sitting reading a comic or eating a sandwich. And Augustine and I will hug him until he can't breathe and tonight we'll have a pizza and cans of pop like we used to when Dad was at home.

We enter the wood and I take the left path. It's cool and dark in here, like always. I can't hear birdsong any more.

It's not far now. Nobody speaks, but I can hear all the tramping boots and rustling uniforms following me.

Sam was always starving when we came to the den. He was hungry all the time.

'Soon, I'm going to get a camping stove in here and some pans,' I told him about a week ago. 'Then we can have a full cooked English breakfast when we come here.'

Sam looked at me doubtfully. 'Where will you get the food from?'

'Out there in the wood. I'm going to make tree-bark bacon, acorn sausages and a leaf smoothie.'

'Ugh!' Sam had laughed. 'You're crackers.'

I laughed too and we had a pretend boxing match. Sam threw a right hook and I acted like he'd knocked me out. When I got back up, I was giggling, but Sam had turned all serious.

'Can this den always be our secret place?' he asked in a small voice.

'Yeah, course it can.'

'I mean, let's promise we never tell anyone else in the world about it. Not even Mum.'

'Promise.' I nodded. 'But when Dad gets out of prison, we might bring him here to show him, yeah? He'll be dead proud of us.'

Sam gave me a weak smile, but didn't say anything.

'We'll have to get another chair for Dad,' I thought aloud. 'But we'll be able to cook him some food on our camping stove. If Dad manages to escape, he can hide out from the police here.'

'Dad's not going to escape, though.'

'You never know. He's a clever man. He told me when I visited him that he was going to escape and that I'd got to—'

'Ed,' Sam had interrupted me. 'Can we just be quiet now?'

I didn't like staying quiet. I didn't like listening

to the thoughts that always started to creep into the silence.

'You OK, Ed?' Augustine squeezes my hand and breaks into my thoughts.

I nod and slow down. 'This is it,' I say, turning round to DI Fenton and pointing to the leaf curtain. 'It's behind there.'

18

I take a step towards the curtain to move it aside when I feel DI Fenton grip my upper arm.

'That's OK, Ed,' he says. 'We'll take it from here. Augustine, can you go with him to wait down the path, please?'

'But I want to see if Sam's in there,' I object.

'Best we do this properly, Ed,' the detective says, glancing at Augustine. 'We'll need to be thorough, get forensics in before everyone tramples around here.'

Augustine nods and we walk past all the officers and stand at the end of the path.

My stomach feels raw. What does he think they might find in there? What if Sam is—

'Don't look so worried,' Augustine interrupts my troubled thoughts. 'They have to dot all the "i"s and cross the "t"s, that's all. Tell you what, though, it sounds like a fine den you've built in there.'

I give her a little smile. 'Sam loves it,' I say in a small voice.

I stand stiff and prickling with nerves as DI Fenton approaches us.

'No sign of Sam in there,' he says. 'Everything neat and

tidy. The community search didn't even find it – you're a master of illusion, Ed.'

I can't speak. My breathing comes short and rapid.

'Are you OK, love?' Augustine grips my shoulders and looks at my face.

'I'm all right,' I manage. 'I just thought . . . I mean, what if Sam had been in there and he was—'

'I know, lad,' DI Fenton says softly. 'But he isn't, and you did a good job bringing us straight here.'

When we get back to the house, the police have moved the ever-growing crowd back a bit.

I ignore the shouted questions, the camera flashes, and I glance past the journalists. I notice the camper-van girl has gone now.

When we step inside the house, I hear Charlie shouting.

'Lorraine doesn't want you here all the time, snooping around and making her feel as if she's hiding something.'

'I'm here to help,' I hear Jill reply. 'To support Lorraine and Ed.'

Augustine pushes open the living-room door.

'What's happening here?'

'Charlie has asked me to leave,' Jill says simply.

'It's not just me.' Charlie glances at Augustine. 'You don't want her here, either, do you, Lorraine?'

Mum looks between Jill and Charlie. She opens her mouth, hesitates.

'Well, tell her, then,' Charlie snaps.

'Thanks, Jill. I know you're only trying to help, but we'll be OK. We can cope.'

I don't want Jill to go. I like her and feel safer knowing she's here and we'll get to know everything that's happening to find Sam.

Jill sighs and hands Mum her card. 'You can reach me any time on this number, Lorraine. If you change your mind—'

'She won't change her mind,' Charlie remarks snidely.

'Lorraine will do what she wants to do.' Everyone looks taken aback at Jill's sharp tone. 'And if I hear about anyone trying to influence her decisions, then I'll be asking some serious questions about certain people's motives.'

Charlie fidgets and coughs. 'Only trying to be supportive,' he mutters.

Jill ignores his comment and turns to me. 'That goes for you too, Ed. If you need anything at all, either ring or come to the station and they'll contact me right away.'

I walk out of the room and climb the stairs. I suddenly feel exhausted, like I could sleep for a month.

The thought of living in a house without Sam, without Jill and without knowing if things will ever be the same again makes me feel like shutting myself away and never coming out to face people again.

I wait until I get to my room before I let the tears come.

DAY TWO

DAY TWO

NOTTINGHAM POST

POLICE TO QUESTION MUM AND NEIGHBOUR OF MISSING LOCAL BOY

Police are to formally question the mother and a neighbour of missing 8-year-old local boy Samuel Clayton today. Officers will also visit HMP Nottingham to speak to Philip Clayton, Samuel's father, currently serving his third year of a ten-year sentence.

An inside source at the prison told the *Post*: 'Phil is beside himself. Nobody from the family had told him about Sam's disappearance. He had to find out through rumour and gossip. He desperately misses his boys.'

The *Post* understands that Mr Clayton has received no visits from his sons or wife for the past fourteen months.

Samuel, known as Sam to family and friends, went missing late on Sunday afternoon while visiting Bulwell Hall Park with his 14-year-old brother. Edward Clayton fell from play equipment and sustained a head injury and still has an incomplete memory of the incident.

Extensive enquiries door-to-door have yielded no suspects, but police say they are still following several leads. Sam has now been missing for 36 hours.

Anyone who has any information about Sam's disappearance should contact Nottinghamshire Police Force confidentially.

It's quiet in the house without the detectives, without Jill. They went home last night. Even the reporters gave up when it got dark, but they're back out there now.

I sit in the armchair by the window. There's a tiny hole here that Dad made when he fell asleep smoking a cigarette.

Mum said it was a miracle she came down to get a glass of water, because otherwise the house could've burned down. As it was, she caught it when it had just started to smoulder.

I push my finger into the hole. The knobbly orange fabric lifts like skin, and my finger presses down into the squashy yellow foam underneath.

I stare at the newspaper again. Someone pushed it through the door this morning and I've read the article five times.

I wonder what Dad's doing right now, this moment. I stopped asking Mum a long time ago about visiting, after she told us that Dad didn't want to see us any more. It was just after Charlie had moved in.

The newspaper article paints a different picture of what Dad wants.

He desperately misses his boys.

What if Mum had told Dad that Sam and I didn't want to see *him*? My tongue feels dry and swollen in my mouth when I think of Dad alone in there, waiting and hoping all this time we might visit.

I hear voices, but it's not the police. Charlie is bringing some of the neighbours inside. They've been desperate to come round since we got home yesterday.

Mum sits down on the settee and covers her face with both hands.

'Come on, love. They're here to help you,' Charlie says. 'Everybody wants to help. They've even brought food and drink, and I, for one, am starving.'

Our neighbours Marg and Arthur are the first ones in.

'We're so sorry for your loss, Lorraine,' Marg says gently.

'He's not *dead*!' Mum's hands fall away from her face and I see her cheeks are bright red. It's not a good sign.

'She just means we're sorry Sam's gone missing,' Arthur remarks. 'Were the boys out on their own again?'

Mum looks away.

Colleen Fischer walks in jiggling Josh, her baby. She puts him outside a lot in his pram and he screams the street down. Sometimes I can hear him crying in the middle of the night from my bedroom window.

Colleen wears short skirts and her legs are always

101

mottled, like corned beef. Arthur sees me looking and winks at me.

'Sorry to hear what's happened, Lorraine,' Colleen says to Mum. 'They're saying he's run off before. Is that true?'

Sylvester walks in quietly. He sits down next to Mum and puts his wrinkled hand on her arm.

His tight curls are all grey now, but once he showed me and Mum a photo of him at a street party taken years ago and he had this cool, massive jet-black Afro.

'He'll turn up,' he says softly to Mum. 'Sam will be home soon, Lorraine. I just know it.'

Mum lays her head gently on Sylvester's shoulder and closes her eyes.

I ignore all the people in our living room and stare out of the window. It's as if coming to our house with all the excitement is something to do for the day. The bottom of the blind is mucky and there are three dead flies on the windowsill, but I like looking out.

I keep hearing words like *abducted* and *pervert* and I start to hum, really quietly, to take my mind off what they're saying.

When I think about where Sam could be right now, it feels like someone is rubbing my skin with one of those green scouring pads Mum uses on dirty saucepans.

He'll be missing his toy cars and the moth-eaten Flopsy Bunny he had from being a baby that he secretly keeps under his pillow. He thinks I don't know, but he falls asleep cuddling it every night.

He acts like he's proper grown up now he's in Year 4 at primary school, but he's still only a baby.

'Now, now, young Edward, why the long face, huh?'

Sylvester is a lovely man, but, like most adults, he can be thick at times.

'My brother going missing might have something to do with it.' I sound snappier than I mean to.

I turn my whole body away from him and stare out of the window, hoping he takes the hint. But he's not put off.

'You know, sometimes, we our own harshest critic,' he says in his soft Jamaican accent. 'We far harder on ourselves than everyone else put together, mon.'

I fidget in my seat, but I don't answer him.

'Everyone here, they are thinking how you must feel. This could have happened to any one of us, at one time or another.'

'It didn't, though, did it?' I keep looking out of the window. 'Stuff like this only happens to *me*.'

Sylvester gives a soft chuckle that cracks like a whip against everyone's worried voices. I turn and glare at him.

'You think you are that special, Ed? The good Lord, he just has it in for you and nobody else in this world, huh?'

He's probably trying to help in his own way, but I don't want to listen to what he has to say any more.

I shuffle to the end of my seat.

'See, when I was around your age, maybe a little younger, we had us a fine young dog.' Sylvester settles back and stares into the middle distance. 'His name was Toby. Followed me everywhere, he did. Like brothers, we were.'

It sounds like one of those Aesop's fables I read as a little kid.

'Anyways, one day me and Toby set off for the market to get some vegetables for my mother when a truck, it come out of nowhere. Knocked little Toby clean off his feet.'

'What happened?'

'He had a real bad limp after that. Took him a long time to get better, but guess what? I tortured myself that it was my fault. I suppose, in a way, it was.'

'But you didn't know the truck would appear out of nowhere,' I say. 'It was just one of those things.'

'That's true. When it happened, I ran for help. Hollering and screaming for anyone and everyone to help Toby.'

When I saw Sam talking to someone in the bushes, I tried to get down to him quick as I could. I wanted to make sure he was safe. I didn't mean to fall and leave him all alone.

'We are not fortune tellers. It is not in our power to know each and every thing that is going to happen in this world,' Sylvester says softly. 'We do our best, you know?'

But the truth is that Toby was a dog, and Sam . . . well, Sam is my brother.

20

When Sylvester has gone home, I sit for a while in the chair, thinking.

'They reckon you've lost your memory,' someone says to my right.

Two boys who live down the road and go to my school have come inside.

I look away. 'Yeah.'

'The police might hypnotize you,' the taller boy says. 'Then you'll be able to remember.'

'I hope they find your brother,' the other one says. 'I hope it's not true what everyone is saying.'

'What's everyone saying?' I ask.

The taller boy's eyes are dancing with excitement. He waves his phone at me.

'See for yourself.'

I take the phone and look at the screen. There's an Instagram photo of Sam on there and someone has super-imposed hearts all over it with the words 'Find Sam'.

'Scroll down,' the boy says. '*That's* what people are saying.'

I read the comments underneath. They start yesterday.

Jon Dumas
@jonny_boy_dumas 17.24

There is something funny going on in that family. Dad in the nick, kids always on their own. #FindSam

Carla Smithson
@carlajanesmithso 17.25

@jonny_boy_dumas Just said the same myself! Bet it turns out to be that family friend, Charlie.

T.J. Don
@TJDon_don_donTJD

@jonny_boy_dumas @carlajanesmithso My neighbour's niece goes to Sam's school & says his older brother is always telling lies.

Marc Brown
@mistermarcusbrown

@TJDon_don_donTJD His brother might know more than he's letting on.

Lisa Cameron
@Ilovejustinbieber

@carlajanesmithso @jonny_boy_dumas It's not fair to be speculating when you don't know the facts. #FindSam

Jon Dumas
@ jonny_boy_dumas

@Ilovejustinbieber Just going on previous cases. Doesn't take much to work out this family are dysfunctional does it?

Ann Lolton
@LittleAnnieLol

@Ilovejustinbieber No good worrying about people's feelings when a kid is missing. Police should be grilling mother, neighbours and the older brother.

Upstairs in my bedroom, I sit curled up where the corner of my bed meets the wall.

I wrap my arms round my knees and stare at the mucky mark on the wall where my head touches. When we moved here, Mum said she'd get the room decorated with superhero wallpaper and everything.

But that was before Dad got sent down.

Our Sam's too young, but I can remember before that, when Dad used to come home every day from work. He didn't get in until late, so we'd have our bath and put our pyjamas on, and then Mum would warm his dinner up and Dad would sit at the table and tell us what had happened that day on the building site.

Dad was a brilliant storyteller, everything so detailed you could see it in your head, like it was right there in front of you.

He told us about his mate Kevin, who'd fallen off some scaffolding and landed with all his weight on one leg.

'Snapped like a cocktail stick, it did,' Dad said with his mouth full of pie and chips. 'The bone poked right out of his shin, and his foot turned round the wrong way, so it was facing behind him. I saw it all with my own eyes.'

'Phil!' Mum scolded him. 'The lads will have nightmares if you carry on. These stories you come back with every day, they're sickening.'

But Dad had just winked at us and waited until Mum went out of the room to tell us even more gory details.

It's not cold in here, but I still shiver.

His brother might know more than he's letting on.

That had been just one of the comments I'd seen on the Instagram feed. That's what people are saying: that I'm a liar, a storyteller, and I haven't lost my memory at all.

Bet it turns out to be that bloke who's always hanging around the family.

Could it be that Charlie has something to do with Sam's disappearance? He's a horrible person. Pretends to be nice when it suits him, but that's just a mask to hide his darker side. But is he really capable of hurting Sam?

It's awful not knowing what's happening with Sam – where he is, if he's safe. But Dad . . . he's stuck at Her Majesty's Pleasure and probably hasn't got a clue what actually happened.

I wish I could see him, talk to him about everything. He'd know what to do.

The house sounds full downstairs. Charlie's put his mate Mick on the door to make sure it's only neighbours coming in and not press.

Loads of the people I saw in the kitchen before I came upstairs don't really know us. They're the people who whisper about Dad behind their hands or cross the road when they see us on the street.

If Mum was feeling her usual self, she wouldn't entertain that lot being in the house. But she isn't her usual self at all. She's letting Charlie do as he likes, as if he lives here and is in charge of us all.

Augustine is around to help, but she has her own house and cats. She can't be here twenty-four/seven.

I haven't heard from Imran again. He's obviously really angry with me. There's nobody else I can talk to.

I hear someone laugh downstairs. My brother has gone, Mum is going crazy, and that idiot Charlie is in the kitchen drinking and laughing with the same people who couldn't stand us yesterday.

I press my fingers into my pocket and pull out the business card that Jill gave me before she left. She'd told me I could call on her at the station, that she was still there for me if I needed anything at all.

I push the idea away, but it won't go. It's getting bigger in my head, growing by the second.

Maybe Jill can help me contact my dad.

I need to work out a way to get out of this house.

21

Dread creeps into the pit of my stomach and pools there like cold sludge.

I've spent the last fifteen minutes wracking my brains for a plan to get out and there's only one thing . . . the worst possible, but the only thing I think will have any chance of working.

I shuffle off the bed, ignoring my thumping head, and focus on praying that for once I get to do the job I hate . . .

I creep downstairs and wait in the hallway for a moment. It's the quietest spot in the house right now. I peek through the door to see a group of the neighbours we know best gathered around my crying mum, offering her words of comfort.

At the kitchen door, it's a different story. Charlie is holding court in front of the people we don't really know.

'So I told all the coppers to get the hell out of the house,' he boasts loudly. 'And if they want to interview me later then they can bloody well wait until *I'm* ready.'

He's not the centre of this tragedy. Nobody wants to speak to *him*.

He looks up sharply, spotting me in the doorway.

'Here he is, man of the moment.' Despite it being early, Charlie swigs beer from a can.

Everybody stops listening to Charlie and stares at me instead.

'It – it's food-bank day,' I falter, hardly believing what I'm about to offer to do. 'I was gonna nip out the back way and get some stuff.'

Charlie's face instantly colours up.

' ? What are you talking about?' He grins at the crowd. 'Losing his marbles, he is. I have nothing to do with places like that, have no need to!'

'But you're the one who told Mum about it in the first place. You said—'

'You're confused. Go back upstairs.' Charlie grasps my arm and leads me to the door and presses some folded-up paper in my hand. 'Don't talk about the food bank in front of this lot,' he hisses. 'Do you want them to think even worse of you?'

In the hallway I unfold the papers. It's a scribbled list from Mum and the food-bank voucher that she gets from Sam's school. The support worker there hands them out to the families that need the extra help.

It's not the actual food bank I'm worried about. It's *after* I've been that the problems can start, when I'm loaded down with all the flimsy white carrier bags. It's hanging around in the doorway of the centre until I'm sure there's nobody around that goes to my school.

That's the stuff that worries me.

A few minutes later, I'm heading out of the house with Mum's scribbled list and the food-bank voucher.

Mixed in with my worries about who might see me at the food bank is the important task of getting in contact with Jill again. Maybe, just maybe, she can help me to get to see Dad.

It's the first time I've been outside on my own since . . . going to the park with Sam. I close my eyes and breathe in fresh air. I feel suffocated in the house with all those people, and Charlie's upbeat mood bothers me. I'm glad to be out of it.

I can hear the buzz of voices out front, but here, in the back yard, there's nobody around, even in the other gardens.

I walk down to the bottom of our overgrown lawn and slip through the broken fence at the bottom. I cut across Mrs Lamb's garden. She's sitting in her chair at the window as usual, and I wave. She's cool about me cutting through.

I dash up the path at the side of her house and a few seconds later I'm on Longford Crescent. There are no press and no police here. In fact, there's nobody around at all.

Perfect.

22

When I get to the police station, I take a deep breath and walk up to the desk. A large man with a badge saying 'Duty Officer' sits behind a plastic screen.

'What can I do for you?' he says, staring at me with deep-set piggy eyes in a sea of pale flesh.

'I'd like to speak to Jill, please . . . She's a family liaison officer.'

He narrows his eyes. 'Are you the boy who . . . ?'

'I'm Ed Clayton,' I say.

He sits up straight then, and I watch as his buttons strain even further against the white cotton of his shirt.

'Yes, course. I thought I recognized you. Take a seat, lad. I'll ring through.'

Five minutes later I'm in a small room with comfy chairs. Sitting across from me is Jill.

'I can't stand Dad having nobody to talk to.' I bite my lip in an effort to stop the tears coming. 'And I need to speak to him. He's the only other person who really understands Sam. Mum does, but she's too upset for me to bother her.'

'I understand,' Jill says. 'Listen, leave it with me and I'll see what I can do.' She slides a small white card across the desk. 'I'll give you my details again. Contact me any time you need to. Now, how are things at home since yesterday?'

'OK,' I say. 'Same as usual in some ways.'

When I leave the station, I feel a bit better, as if things might move on a bit now Jill is involved again. She couldn't make any promises about seeing Dad, but it's a start. Even the thought of having to go to the food bank seems a bit less daunting. Until I see Bulwell Academy on the other side of the road, that is . . .

My shoulders tensed as I walked into the classroom. Most people were already seated and I relaxed a bit when I saw Miss Morton was already at the front of the class.

At least they couldn't do anything too bad to me.

'Ah, there you are, Ed. Nice of you to join us at last.'

'He's been busy scavenging in the bins, miss,' a familiar voice piped up from the back row one morning. 'For his breakfast.'

A wave of sniggering rose and fell in the room as Miss Morton stalked down to Aidan.

'One more comment like that and you're straight to the head. Is that clear?'

Aidan nodded sullenly. 'Whatever, miss.'

I pulled out a chair at the end of the row and sat down next to Martha Penn.

'So we're looking at Of Mice and Men *this morning.'* Miss Morton returned to her desk. 'Textbooks out, please.'

Before I even stuck my hand into my rucksack, I remembered I'd left the book under my bed. And I hadn't done the reading we were supposed to do on the Great Depression, either. I took out my pencil case and ruler and an old maths book I had in there, hoping it would be enough to fool her.

'Where's your book?' Martha hissed at me.

Martha Penn's hair was matted at the back and she smelled of warm, stale biscuits.

'Mind your own business,' I hissed back, but it was too late. Miss Morton looked across and her eyes scanned the desk in front of us.

'Where's your textbook, Ed?'

'He's eaten it, miss!'

'That's enough, Aidan,' Miss Morton snapped before asking me again. 'Your book, Ed?'

'I dropped it this morning, miss, when I walked to school.'

'And . . . did you pick it up again?'

'I couldn't, miss. It – it fell down a drain.'

Hoots of laughter sounded from the back of the room.

'Your book fell down a drain?'

'Yes, miss.'

'I see. It would be nigh on impossible for a book to fall

115

down a drain, wouldn't it? A key, perhaps, or a pen . . . but a textbook, Ed?'

'It fell at exactly the right angle and just slipped down there, miss.'

'Looks like half your trousers fell down there, an' all!'

I scooted my feet under the chair to hide my short trousers. I'd forgotten to remind Mum to look in the charity shop for a new pair at the beginning of term.

Behind me, the laughter of the back rows nipped at my reddening ears. I prayed the heat wouldn't spread into my face, but it didn't work.

Miss Morton clapped her hands short and sharp. 'That's enough!'

She glanced at my legs under the chair and smiled kindly. 'Are you OK, Ed?'

'Yes, miss!' I ignore the heavy weight that's settled on my chest and focus on keeping my voice bright. 'I've got brand-new school trousers at home. I just don't want to wear them yet.'

'Liar, liar, pants on fire!' the familiar chant began at the back of the room.

I thought I could make things better by saying the right thing. But like always, it just got worse.

I looked up the dictionary definition of the word 'poor' once.

'Lacking sufficient money to live at a standard considered comfortable or normal in society.'

I reckon the person who wrote that definition has never been poor.

Otherwise they'd know that *poor* is like a layer of grease floating on water. No matter how hard you try to shake it off, it won't go away and it won't mix in.

Poor sticks to your skin and everyone can see it, even when you try to cover it up.

Poor is being afraid to go into certain shops because somehow the assistants *just know* you can't afford anything on the shelves. It's finding something you urgently need to do when your classmates are excitedly planning to go to the cinema and then the bowling alley on Saturday. It's pushing your feet right back under the chair so nobody spots the peeling soles on your third-hand trainers.

Poor is pretending you're not hungry when others are going to McDonald's after school.

After a while, *poor* just becomes who you are.

23

It takes me about ten more minutes to get to the food bank. When I'm near, I slow down and peer round the corner.

The food bank is a charity, run by the church, and operates out of the community hall three times a week. It opens at twelve, but there's a drop-in cafe every morning from 9 a.m. where people in need can get a free breakfast and a hot drink.

There's ten minutes still to go before the food bank itself opens and there's already a queue.

My heart thumps hard on my chest wall. There's a big lump in my throat that's made up of chunks of different things. It's hard to separate them all out.

I pull my baseball cap down a bit lower and scan the people in the queue. It's not just old people, or young people, or mothers with pushchairs, or young men tapping on their phones, or old men leaning on their sticks . . . it's *all* of them.

I guess there's not a 'type' that comes here.

There is no one I recognize and I'm grateful that, despite Sam's disappearance being on the local news and in the newspapers, nobody has recognized me, either.

I join the end of the queue. A couple of people glance at me, but most don't seem to notice anything at all, preferring to stare at their own feet. That is, apart from a scruffy-looking girl standing with her dad who, from the back, looks like she hasn't combed her hair any time in the last three years.

She turns round and gives me a little smile and I look quickly away as heat flushes into my face and I realize with horror that . . . she is the new girl next door.

At exactly noon, the sound of bolts sliding back gets the queue shuffling and, finally, the community-centre doors are opened.

'Morning,' a plump woman with curly brown hair and black-rimmed spectacles says. I think her name is Maureen. A couple of people grunt back, but I don't say anything.

I just want it to be over.

The queue starts to file in slowly like a reluctant caterpillar. We all feel the same . . . nobody really wants to be here, but we're grateful for it all the same.

I hear laughter behind me and I spin round, ready to come up with a convincing excuse as to why I'm here, but it's just boys on bikes and I don't know any of their faces.

The queue inches forward and, finally, I find myself at the entrance desk. I hand over the voucher to the lady sitting there.

'Are you on your own again, pet?' she asks in a broad north-east accent.

'Yeah,' I say. 'My mum's broken her ankle, so it's really difficult for her to get down here.'

She looks at me and does a double-take.

'Oh, it's you . . . I mean, hello, love. Let's help you get sorted out.' She bites her lip as if she's concerned and calls over to the lady who opened the doors. 'Maureen, this young man is on his own. Could you help him, please?'

The people in the queue behind me look me up and down a bit as if they're trying to work out why I'm the only kid who's on his own in the queue and why the ladies are fussing over me.

I look at the wall, so they can't see my face. I don't want them to know who I am. I don't want to answer any questions or be subjected to their sympathies.

I just want to disappear.

Maureen grabs a couple of white plastic shopping bags. 'What's your name, ducky?'

'Ed,' I mumble.

'Right. I thought so.' I follow her over to the stacked shelves and she suddenly turns to me and whispers, 'Look, I know who you are and what's happened with your brother and I just want to say we all feel very bad for you here. And if you need anyone to talk to, then—'

'Thanks,' I interrupt her, willing her to just stop. And she gets it.

'OK. So let's start with the tins, then, Ed. I'll tell you what we've got, and you tell me if you want it. OK?'

'OK. I've got a list here from my mum.' I hand over the note. 'She says I have to get everything that's on it.'

'I see.' She takes the paper from me. 'Well, we'll certainly do our very best. First item on the list is baked beans, so that's easy enough.'

She drops two large tins into a bag.

'Tomato soup and a loaf of bread. Bread's frozen, is that OK?' I nod and hold the bag and she loads it with more items. 'So your mum's broken her ankle, I heard you say. How did she manage that?'

I make a thing of reading the back of a packet of sage-and-onion stuffing mix.

'Ed . . . I was asking about your mum?'

'Sorry.' I place the packet back on the metal shelving unit. 'She slipped while she was . . .' I look around wildly and my eyes settle on the loo door in the corner. 'While she was on the toilet.'

'Heavens!' Maureen's eyes widen and she stops putting stuff in the bag. 'She slipped while she was actually *on* the toilet, you say? That must be pretty difficult to do. What happened?'

'She sat down on the loo and saw something horrible move on the floor and she jumped up, tripped and fell off the toilet.'

'Sounds very painful. And with everything else

that must be going on in your house. What was it that moved?'

'A snake. It had escaped from a neighbour's house.'

'Good gracious!' Maureen clutches at her throat. 'Was it a big one?'

'It was an anaconda,' I say, getting into my stride now. 'Same as the ones in *Snakes on a Plane*. In fact, there were three of them. Three man-eating anacondas, on our bathroom floor.'

I hear a snigger and catch the girl in the queue watching us from the other side of the shelving unit. I turn my back to her.

'I see,' Maureen says, less convinced now. She presses her lips together as if she's trying not to smile. 'Man-eating snakes are usually only found in tropical climates, if I'm not mistaken . . . except in stories, of course.' The bottom of my back feels hot. 'Ed, it's OK. You don't have to make up—'

'Mum said we need some butter this time too,' I say quickly.

She sighs.

'Your mum knows there's no refrigeration here and we can't stock certain foods without it.'

'Oh,' I say.

Maureen doesn't ask me anything else about Mum after that, and I'm glad.

24

I take the two bulging bags full of food and thank Maureen for her help.

'You're welcome, Ed. And remember what I said . . . If you need to talk, we're all friends here.'

I feel bad making up stories when she was only asking after Mum's wellbeing. But what could I do? Every time they comment I'm on my own again, I think this might be the time they turn me away.

I reach the foyer and wait at the door, looking up and down the street.

There's an old fella chugging along on his mobility scooter, but apart from him the coast is clear. I slip out of the community centre and begin to walk away briskly.

I keep my chin tucked into my chest as my eyes scan the road ahead. My throat feels really dry.

'Hey! Hold up,' a girl's voice calls behind me. 'Ed!'

I stop and turn round. It's the girl from next door who was eavesdropping at the food bank. I can feel my forehead creasing into a frown.

I adjust the bags and take a couple of steps away, but

then I hear her rapid footsteps and breathlessness behind me.

'Do you know what *hold up* means, or are you deaf?' she scolds as she draws level with me. 'It means *wait*, not flipping storm off.'

She has a soft Irish accent that would be quite nice to listen to if she wasn't being so irritating.

'I'm in a rush,' I say curtly. 'Plus, I don't even know you.'

'Everybody seems to know you, judging by the crowd of folks outside your front gate.'

The thin plastic handles of the bags are cutting into my fingers, so I put them down for a second or two.

'That's because my brother is missing,' I tell her.

'I know. It must be awful for your family. Sorry.' She holds out a small, pale hand. 'My name is Fallon Twigg.'

'Oi, Clayton, you stinking scrounger!'

My hand freezes in mid-air.

Fallon's head whips round and I look down at my feet.

'Look, let's go back to the cafe and have a glass of juice or something,' Fallon suggests when she spots the group of lads.

'Clayton! Giz a bag of food-bank crisps, will ya?' one of them calls.

My head starts to pound. It's definitely Aidan's voice. He still sounds quite a way off.

'Maybe he's *lost* the food-bank crisps . . . like he lost his brother!' Laughter and whistling follows.

'Come on,' Fallon urges me, turning back to the building.

Reluctantly, I follow her back inside.

'Friends of yours, are they?' Fallon remarks.

I shrug. 'Used to be.'

There are a few tables spare.

'Sit down,' Fallon says. 'Orange cordial?'

I nod.

'Hungry?'

'Nah, thanks,' I say, and I realize that my appetite has disappeared since Sam went.

There's some banging on the entrance-door glass and someone presses their face up to the window, squashing his features against it. Bailey.

The people in the cafe give a cursory glance and then get back to chatting. They've seen worse, no doubt.

Bailey's face disappears as they all move on. Seems they haven't the courage to come in here. After all, poor people are a different, dangerous breed.

A grandma with a baby in a pushchair walks by me and stops dead.

'Are you that boy who . . .' She peers closer. 'It is you, isn't it? How are you, love? I'm so sorry to hear what happened. God bless you and your family.'

'Thanks,' I mutter.

'Who was that?' Fallon reappears with two glasses of juice and watches the woman leave.

'Dunno,' I say, pulling up my fleece collar and tugging down my hat even further. 'But she was nice, asking about our Sam.'

I push my chair round so my back is to the room. Fallon sits opposite me and I notice, for the first time, that she has one green eye and one blue. Her skin is pale and her dreadlocks a deep, dark red.

She smiles at a young couple with a toddler on the next table.

'Have you been here before?' I ask her. She seems to have no shame or embarrassment in being here.

She throws her head back and lets out a hearty laugh. She has a missing molar at the side.

She makes me feel like a daft kid.

'What happened to your tooth?' I ask, hoping to embarrass her.

'My mam got drunk one day and knocked it out,' she said easily. 'It's one of the reasons Dad left her.'

I can't believe she's just told me something as personal as that. I try to think of a smart reply, but I can't.

'How did you already know my name?' I say instead.

'I overheard you say it when you checked in with the food-bank receptionist. You have a loud voice . . . Anyone ever tell you that?'

I don't answer her.

'Oh, and there's the small matter of half the country's newspapers camped outside your house.' Her voice softens a little. 'I'm really sorry about your brother, Ed. I hope they find him soon.'

A ribbon of guilt twirls in my stomach as Sam's face drifts into my mind.

'So, how long you been coming to the food bank, then?' She brightens her voice a bit, looking to change the subject. 'The staff seem really nice in there.'

'Oh, I go to the food bank for my mum's friend, Augustine,' I say smoothly, nodding to the bags. 'All this stuff is for her.'

Fallon widens her eyes. 'Really? Well, me and Dad go to the food bank for ourselves. This stuff is for *us*.'

'Was that your dad you were with in there?' I'm not sure why I've started up the conversation again.

'Yeah, his name's Pat. Short for Patrick. He's not too bad, as far as parents go, that is.'

'You're very . . . *honest*, aren't you? I mean, about your mum and your dad.' *Blunt* would be a better word.

'Why not? It's the truth.' She shrugs. 'Know what that is, do you? *Truth*?'

'What's that supposed to mean?'

I bet people have been gossiping to her already. The reporters and neighbours, talking about me on the street.

His older brother is always telling lies. That's what one

127

of the Instagram comments had said on the feed about Sam.

'Erm . . . it might have something to do with that fascinating tale of how three man-eating anacondas scared your mum off the bog.' She laughs again.

'You should mind your own business.' I can feel my face burning. 'I wasn't even talking to *you*.'

'I like writing,' she says grandly, flicking her dreadlocks this way and that. 'And writers get their material by listening in to other people's conversations. Don't you know anything?'

It feels like something is building in my chest, ready to burst out.

Her face grows serious. 'Is it all true, Ed . . . the stuff the newspapers are saying?'

'Some of it, I suppose.' I breathe out. 'But some of it is lies.'

'Which bit is true?'

'That I can't remember anything about how exactly Sam went missing.' I want to stop there, but I feel my face darken. 'Some of what *they're* saying is lies, though, and, well, they're bringing up stuff that's not relevant. They're the liars.'

'Why do you think they lie?'

'Who knows? Probably because they don't like the boring truth.' I scowl. 'They want to make things more exciting than they really are and it's far easier to make things up than to face the truth, isn't it?'

Fallon tips her head to one side and studies me for a moment.

'Hmm,' is all she says.

25

We leave the cafe once Aidan and the others are gone.

Soon we get to the end of Longford Crescent.

'I need to use a shortcut across the gardens to get back on to Grindon,' I tell her. 'So *they* don't spot me.'

'Cool. I don't want to walk by them either, so I'll use the shortcut with you.'

'See you around, yeah?' she says when we get home.

I give her a little nod and run up the garden.

Soon as I open the back door, Charlie appears. The kitchen is empty of the so-called guests now.

'What took you so long? We're bloody starving here.' He snatches one of the bags from me.

'There was a long queue,' I tell him, wondering why he's still hanging around our house and not back in his own. 'The lady had to take me round.'

'Long queue my arse.' Charlie frowns. 'I saw you out of the window, talking to one of those flea-ridden hippies who've just moved in next door.'

'Her name's Fallon.' I put the other bag on the countertop. 'She's moved here with her dad.'

Mum appears in the doorway, flanked by Augustine.

'You shouldn't have gone out, Ed,' Mum says. Her voice

sounds weak, and her worn, shabby clothes are bagging round her wrists and waist. 'The press would've eaten you alive if they'd seen you.'

'No use wrapping him in cotton wool, Lorraine,' Charlie grumbles. 'He made sure *he* was safe and sound when Sam was in danger, didn't he?'

'Charlie!' Augustine snaps at him, and he closes his mouth. She smiles at me. 'Just to let you know, love, we've had a chat and I'm going to be sort of moving in here – during the day, anyway. I'll do the cooking and look after your mum.'

This is good news. I just hope it doesn't mean Charlie is going to be around here more too.

'I'll sleep at mine, of course, and keep popping back over the road to feed the cat and stuff, but it should make things a bit easier here in the house.'

I nod my approval. Since Charlie sent Jill away, there's been nobody to keep things on a level here, and I don't know how long Mum can hold up without help.

Charlie rummages around in the bags.

'So, where's the milk, the cheese and the butter? Have you scoffed it or summat?'

I look at him.

'They don't stock that sort of stuff because they have no fridges there.'

Charlie seems to think it's like going to Sainsbury's, that we can have every single item we ask for.

'*No fridges?*' Charlie looks thoughtful. 'There are people down the pub think those places dole out absolutely everything to people who just can't be bothered to work.'

'If I could work, I'd be out there in a jiffy, earning,' Mum says faintly.

'We know you'd work, Lorraine,' Charlie says. 'But not everyone is like you. Some folks just expect handouts.'

'I've never met anyone who wants to rely on a food bank for long, but it's a godsend in hard times,' Mum says. 'Maybe you should tell your mates it's a helping hand when folks need it, not a lifestyle choice.'

'If people just stopped to think what they're saying and stopped repeating the lies they read in the gutter press, we'd all be better off.' Augustine frowns at Charlie.

I find myself wondering why we're arguing about what other people think of us when Sam is still missing, while he's out there somewhere, alone and afraid. And why it's OK for the papers to lie, but nobody else can.

That's when it strikes me that the adults aren't really getting anywhere. For all the questioning, the searching and the pondering, they're no closer to finding Sam.

Nobody has really asked about Sam himself. How he thinks, what he likes to do, where he might like to go.

I'm the only person who *really* knows how Sam's mind works.

Mum and Augustine are watching me. Their mouths

are moving, their brows are furrowed, but I feel like I'm underwater.

Once, when we went on a school trip to the Lace Market, we climbed right up to St Mary's bell tower. We wore ear protectors, but when the bells rang it sounded so loud that the vibrations filled not just your head but your whole body.

I can't hear what Mum and Augustine are saying – all I can hear is a tinny echo. All I can feel is the pain of being without my brother.

I'll have to find him myself.

26

'Fancy coming round for a cup of chai?' Fallon says over the low fence that separates our two houses.

I look up from where I'm sitting on the kitchen step. '*Chai?*'

'Indian tea,' she says, as if I ought to already know. 'It's warm and spicy.'

Fallon waits for my reply, her lips twitching in amusement.

Behind me, through the closed door, I can hear the raised voices of Mum and Charlie in the kitchen.

'OK.' I walk across the lawn and vault over the waist-high fence.

The garden this side is even more neglected than ours, if that's possible. The lawn is long, but you can't see any borders, and even the grass is being choked out by weeds.

The house is the same as ours from the outside, but some time ago it was converted into four small flats by the council.

'We're upstairs,' Fallon says, leading the way up some side steps.

When we step inside, the fusty smell of damp hits me

right away. We have damp in our house too, but I think this particular flat has been vacant for a while.

I follow her through the small hallway and into the living room overlooking the road.

'This is Neil, my dad.'

Neil is sitting cross-legged on the floor, eyes closed . . . but upside down *in a headstand*.

'Blimey!' I gasp.

'Dad's into yoga. And he drinks a lot of chai tea.' Fallon grins. '*Dad!*'

His eyes open and he smiles.

'This is Ed, from next door. You know, the boy I told you about.'

Neil unfurls his legs and slides gracefully into standing. He's tall. Very tall.

'Pleased to meet you, mate,' he says. 'Sorry to hear about your troubles.' He tips his head back towards the press outside our gate.

'Hello,' I say, shaking his hand.

Now I see where Fallon got her different-coloured eyes from and her red hair. Neil's hair is wavy and touches his shoulders.

'Any news yet . . . about your brother?' he asks.

I shake my head.

'Ed's come round here for a bit of peace,' Fallon says, squeezing my arm. 'And for a cup of your famous chai.'

'Now you're talking!' Neil's face breaks into a grin

again. 'Sit down, then. Make yourself comfy. I'll bring it through.'

Instead of sitting, I walk over to the window and look down on the crowd. It seems to have thinned out just a little. Are they already losing interest in Sam?

It's strange seeing things from a different angle, like all the neighbours must be doing. To look at someone else's drama and be OK in your own life.

Fallon joins me at the glass. 'They don't give up, do they?'

'No,' I agree. 'But I look at them and I'm glad they're there, reminding everyone Sam is still missing.'

'What do you mean?'

'Well, nothing seems to be happening. I think it'd go quiet without them. The police ring every couple of hours to update Mum – Augustine usually takes the call because Mum is finding it hard to focus at the moment – and they say they're *doing this, doing that*, but they don't seem to be getting any closer to finding Sam.'

Fallon purses her lips. 'I suppose it takes time.'

'But they know *nothing about Sam*, what kind of a person he is, how he might react to being lost or alone or . . .' I falter. I don't want to voice some of the awful things that might've happened to him. 'I wish *I* was in charge of the flipping investigation.'

'Why? What would you do?' Fallon asks, looking at me.

136

'Dunno. I'd start by going back to the park and tracking all the places we used to go . . . just like they're doing, I suppose.' I wince as my fingernails dig into my palms. 'I don't know, I just feel so hopeless, sitting here, reading stories in the papers and worrying about Sam and Dad . . .'

My words tail off. I didn't mean to mention Dad.

'Do you still see your dad, Ed?' Fallon has got this annoying way of just asking stuff without worrying whether it seems rude or nosy.

The cogs start whirring in my head and the best story about Dad's absence presents itself. It's the one I usually use with people: Dad is working abroad, running a very successful company that makes loads of money. The downside is I don't get to see him much, but that will all change in the future when I go to live with him . . .

I open my mouth to repeat it, but something weird happens. Something in the way she looks at me makes me bite back the words, and I sense her reaction will be the same whether she gets the story or the truth.

In a split second, I decide to take a crazy chance.

'Dad's in prison,' I say softly.

A noise behind me interrupts the moment.

'Your dad's in prison?' Neil appears with a floral tray and three small steaming cups set on it.

I swallow and the words come before I even stop to think.

'No! Well, not really.' The newspaper headline bounces around in my head. Neil might have already seen it.

'I mean, technically he *is* in prison at the moment, but he's getting out really soon to help us look for Sam.'

'Oh, that's good news,' Neil says, walking over to us. 'Tough for you and your family, though, him being inside.'

He offers me the tray and I take a cup without answering. He probably won't want me hanging around with Fallon now he knows Dad's banged up. Who can blame him?

'I visit him and write to him every week.' I'm speaking too fast, but I can't stop. I just want to make things better.

Neil looks at me. 'That's cool. It was different for me. I really missed my dad and hardly ever got to visit him. Didn't stop me thinking about him all the time, though.'

I blink.

'I used to wear his sweatshirt all the time.' Neil smiles at the memory. 'Daft, really. I was only twelve and it was far too big for me. Falling to bits, it was, but I wouldn't let my mum wash it. It kept Dad's smell for ages. Used to make me feel he was still around, you know?'

I nod, thinking about how I keep Dad's beanie hat in my drawer. I've never told anyone that.

'I . . . I've never met anyone else before whose dad went to prison,' I say slowly. 'I thought—'

'Thought that you were the only one?'

I nod.

'Yeah, me too. I felt like I was the only kid in the world whose dad was locked away, but guess what? There are two hundred and fifty thousand children in the UK who have a parent in prison.'

My mouth falls open.

'It's a big number, right? There's not just you, Ed. Remember that.'

Neil gulps down his drink and walks across the room.

'Right. I'm off to my yoga class. See you both later.'

'Bye, Dad,' Fallon calls. 'We're stony broke at the moment, but Dad's setting up some yoga classes.' Fallon smiles proudly. 'Hopefully things will get easier soon.'

I sense that Fallon sees the bright side of things, even when life isn't great.

I inhale the steam from the cup and take a sip of the creamy chai. It is fragrant and spicy and it instantly warms up my insides.

So does the thought that there are thousands of other kids out there somewhere who are missing their mum or dad, just like me.

27

'I've been thinking about what you said,' Fallon says when we've finished our tea. 'You know, about how you wish you could be in charge of the police investigation.'

'Yeah.' I give a short bitter laugh. 'Fat chance of that, though.'

'Agreed. But what if you started your own investigation? I mean, aside from the official police one, obviously. Like you said, you know Sam better than anyone else.'

I open my mouth, ready to give her a hundred reasons why it won't work, but I can't actually think of a single one.

'What harm will it do?' Fallon's voice rises an octave as she gathers momentum. 'I can help you! We won't be interfering in anything the police are doing. We can draw up a bit of a plan now and just see how it goes.'

She looks at me, her eyes sparking in anticipation of my reply.

A tiny flicker starts up inside my chest. Anything would be better than just sitting here doing nothing. But then the worries begin.

'Mum – the police – they won't like us doing anything

on our own . . . and how can we investigate without the press finding out?'

'You're *here* without them knowing, aren't you?' Fallon remarks. 'And you went to the food bank unnoticed. Thanks to your shortcuts across the estate.'

'They recognized me there, though.'

'You just need a better disguise – that's all. Wrap a scarf around your mouth and borrow a different jacket. My dad has a couple in his wardrobe. I can help you with that too.'

'OK,' I say slowly, warming to the idea. 'I suppose we could *try*, at least.'

'That's the spirit.' Fallon claps her hands. 'I'll get a pen and paper.'

Twenty minutes later, we sit together and stare at the list Fallon has made.

PLAN TO FIND SAM
Retrace steps
Visit den
Visit Dad
Sam's stuff

'Maybe . . . ' I hesitate. 'Maybe we should add Charlie's name to that list.'

'Why's that?' Fallon looks up.

'Dunno, just that he's not really acting normal. He's

showing off a lot and being even more arrogant than usual. I think he's too stupid to know anything about Sam going missing, but taking a bit of a closer look at him won't hurt.'

'OK,' Fallon agrees and picks up her pen again to add Charlie to the list. 'Can't do any harm and I agree he certainly seems a bit involved in you and your mum's lives to say he's just a neighbour.'

'It doesn't look like much of an investigation.' I sigh. 'All this stuff has already been done apart from "visit Dad". The police and community search covered the park and the den, and they've searched our room.'

'But *you* haven't done it personally,' Fallon reminds me. 'It might help jog your memory and, as you've said, you know Sam best. So maybe the police missed something. Who knows.'

'It's a start,' I agree. 'And it's better than waiting and hoping and doing nothing.'

'Exactly.' Fallon nods. 'Now, let's get your disguise sorted.'

'Are you sure your dad won't mind?' I feel uncomfortable, standing in Neil's bedroom as Fallon rifles through his wardrobe.

'Nah, he hasn't worn this for ages, anyway.' She holds up a denim jacket. 'Sorry it's a bit dated.'

I laugh. 'Not sure if you've noticed, but my wardrobe isn't full of designer gear, either.'

'Yeah, I suppose.' She pauses. 'Have things always been this tough for you – I mean, as they are now – using the food bank and stuff?'

I think for a moment and realize that I've got used to money being scarce, but life used to be different when Dad was still around . . .

I piled out of class with everyone else and lifted my face up to the sun. I loved Fridays!

'You coming down the field tonight?' Aidan caught up with me. 'Game of footie and then chip shop afterwards?'

'Nah, not tonight,' I told him. 'Family movie and pizza night cos Dad's finishing work early.'

'Sounds good. Fancy coming to my house on Saturday, then? We're overdue for a serious Xbox session.'

'You're on!' I grin. 'Dad's going to buy me one for my birthday, then you'll be able to come around mine sometimes too.'

'Cool. See you tomorrow, then, mate.'

'So much has changed since Dad went to prison,' I say to Fallon. 'It's not just money – it's friends, neighbours, Mum's health . . . You expect life to carry on as normal, but it doesn't. Nothing is the same.'

'Sounds like you're all being punished, as well as your dad.'

'Yeah, feels like that a lot of the time.'

'I don't know how you cope with it, but I suppose you have no choice but to get on with it,' Fallon says softly. 'Or pretend to yourself it's not happening.'

I know what she's getting at.

'It's hard to accept the truth,' I say. 'Sometimes it feels like I'll do and say anything just to escape it. I just find myself saying what I'd like things to be like or telling a silly story – like the one about the snakes – to distract from the truth. Half the time I don't even know I'm doing it.'

Fallon thinks for a moment. 'I think I understand why you do it and at least you admit to knowing you do it.'

I smile, pleased she seems to be agreeing with me.

'But then you'll also know that telling lies doesn't work. When the stories have been told, the truth is still waiting for you just the same. Right?'

28

When I get back home, Mum and Augustine look flustered, and Charlie is pale and quiet as he pulls on a denim jacket.

'It's time for Charlie to go down the station.' Mum wrings her hands together. 'The police are coming now to take him in for questioning.'

'And everyone knows I'm being questioned thanks to that flipping newspaper announcing it. Persecution, that's what it is,' Charlie mutters to himself. 'They've no leads, you see, so they're coming after me. I told them everything I know, yesterday.'

His eyes are wild and his face has a sheen to it. He actually looks scared. Could he have anything to hide?

I can't imagine that Charlie has hurt Sam, not really. But it just shows Fallon was right to include it on the list and, after his drinking and socializing with the neighbours this morning, I can't help feeling glad the smile has been wiped off Charlie's face at last. Maybe it's because he's gone to the papers, even though Jill and the police told him not to.

He sees me looking and glares back. I don't want an argument. I'm still feeling hopeful after chatting to Fallon about our plans.

Before anyone can stop me, I run upstairs and slam my door behind me. When I look around, the bedroom still seems so different. Empty.

Without Sam, it's just not home any more.

I lean on the windowsill and stare out.

I can see across the rooftops to St Mary's Church in the distance. If I had wings, I could open the long window right now and just go. Soar over all the crap, get away from the whispers and the accusing stares downstairs.

Even though our house is crabby and small, when I sit here my head fills with air and space. I feel like I can breathe again.

Looking across the red rooftops, I listen to my stomach rumbling and feel like I'm ready to crumple into myself like a screwed-up piece of paper. The pressure, the worry, the wondering . . . it's like a great weight that's hovering over my head, about to crush me at any moment.

I cover my face with my hands and try to take some deep breaths, but that doesn't do any good. Without even meaning to, I start to build a story in my mind . . .

Dad once told me that his mum and dad, mine and Sam's grandparents, emigrated to Australia when Dad was in his early twenties. He'd never been out there to see them, but said he hoped one day they'd come back to live in the UK.

He talked to them on the phone about three times a year, and once he held the phone to my mouth so I could say hello.

What if they came to the door right now to tell us they have Sam and they're going to take me and Mum too, to live in their big posh house with a proper driveway. No more trips to the food bank, and Mum could come off her tablets and stop sleeping all afternoon because she'd have nothing to worry about any more. Dad would get out of prison early and . . .

Who am I kidding? Why do I make this stuff up?

It feels like my heart is sinking into my abdomen. These stupid stories aren't doing any good at all. They aren't making anything better in the real world.

Sam is missing and we don't know what's happened to him.

That's the awful truth that can't be tweaked into a happy-ever-after tale, no matter how hard I try.

But if Dad was here he wouldn't sit at home wondering what the police were doing. He'd be out there, searching everywhere for Sam. I just know it.

About six months before Dad got arrested, we went for a walk down by the canal, just the two of us.

He didn't say too much at first, but he was acting a bit strangely, like he was trying to stop some secret excitement from getting out. He had this sort of half-smile on his face.

'Are you OK, Dad?' I asked after we'd been walking a while.

He picked up a stone from the towpath and skimmed it across the water. I stopped walking and skimmed one too.

'I think mine went further,' I teased, and he nudged me.

I started to walk again, but Dad stayed put. He stared out at the water, his hands in his pockets. We stood like that for a bit without speaking.

'Do you reckon you could keep a secret, Ed?' Dad's voice sounded tight and high like he wasn't sure whether to say the words out loud or not.

'Course,' I said.

'I've met someone, a business partner who wants us to work together. But not as an employee, as a proper director, like.' Dad puffed out his chest.

'What sort of business is it?' I asked him.

He paused and then carried on talking as if I hadn't said anything.

'They've never trusted anybody enough before. Too many people wanting to screw them over, you know?' He looked across to the other side of the canal. 'I've been waiting for an opportunity like this.'

Dad used to work as a joiner, but one day he came home and told us they'd made him redundant. Him and

Mum used to argue about it. But if me and Sam were around, they'd do it quietly, in whispers.

Dad said it was important Mum didn't find out about the business opportunity.

'Until I've made a bit of money and she can see it's a good move,' he explained.

'Are you going to work with this person, then?' I asked him.

'Yeah, I think so.' Dad grinned and put his hand on my shoulder. It felt heavy and warm through my fleece. 'Let's sit here and have our picnic, shall we?'

We sat on a wooden bench. One of the slats had snapped at one end, so we shuffled up closer together.

Dad pulled a carrier bag from his rucksack. He took out a foil-wrapped square and handed it to me.

I unwrapped it and took out one half of the white bread-and-butter sandwich.

'Not much, I know.' Dad gave me a handful of crisps. 'But when I get sorted out there'll be plenty of proper sandwiches with ham and cheese on, I promise you.'

A burst of chatter downstairs from the kitchen drifts up to the bedroom like a wisp of smoke, and the past dissolves into nothing again.

29

At teatime, Mum goes across the road to have her bath at Augustine's – we haven't got enough on the electric card for that much hot water.

Five minutes later, Charlie walks in.

'Mum's not here,' I say, but he sits down anyway and starts crowing.

'Police had to let me go. See, they can't pin anything on an innocent man, no matter how hard they try.'

He seems so pleased with himself . . . almost as if he *has* got something to hide, but the police haven't been able to find it.

Too pleased, despite the fact that soon Sam will have been missing for forty-eight hours.

'What's the sour face for?' he sneers.

'My brother is still missing,' I say. 'I don't see any reason to feel happy.'

'And who's fault is *that*?' he shoots back immediately.

I want to run upstairs, but I don't. My dad would punch his lights out if he could, but he's got another seven years to serve.

'This is all *your* fault,' he says quietly, a smirk curling up the corners of his thin, colourless lips. 'You're a bit useless, really, aren't you? Just like your old man. Between you, you'll drive your mother down again – you'll see.'

The images of Mum's *bad time* when Dad got arrested flood back into my mind. There was literally no money coming into the house that winter until Mum got her cleaning job.

Mum started turning off the Christmas food adverts. It was only thanks to the food bank that we got a turkey dinner on Christmas Day. It really hit her hard.

Coming in from school every day with Mum in bed, listless and empty. Making Sam's tea with whatever I could find and trying to keep the house tidy for when Mum felt better.

Then one day looking in her bedroom and seeing her lying there, still and grey in the face like a dead fish. One glassy eye half open, one closed. Running over the road to Augustine's house and waiting while she rang 999.

Mum was OK. She'd forgotten she'd already taken her tablets and had double-dosed by accident.

There's a knock at the back door.

'If that's those bloody coppers again, they'll get short shrift from me.' Charlie springs to his feet and stomps into the kitchen. 'Oh, it's *you*,' I hear him say.

Fallon comes in the room. I feel a flush of heat rising and my heartbeat speeds up.

'Just came over to see how you are, Ed,' she says easily, standing by the door.

'As you can see, he's fine,' Charlie shouts from the kitchen. 'Loving all the attention.'

'Man, it's freezing in here.' She's wearing a sleeveless T-shirt, showing off pale, freckled skin.

'The boiler's broken again,' I hear myself say.

Charlie smirks at Fallon as he walks in carrying a cup of tea he's made for himself.

There are a few moments of silence and I realize Fallon looks a bit uncomfortable just stood there.

'Sit down if you want,' I say.

'Thanks.' She plonks herself down on the settee. 'So, when's your heating getting fixed?'

Charlie looks up from his phone. 'Nowt up with the heating as far as I know.'

My heart starts thumping again.

'I thought you said the boiler was broken, Ed?' Fallon looks puzzled.

'I – I thought it was.' I clamp my mouth shut before I dig myself in even deeper.

'They can't afford to put the heating on.' Charlie sniffs. 'You've only just moved here, so you don't know he's a big fat liar. I wouldn't trust him to tell me what day it was.'

'Oh well, no harm done.' Fallon smiles brightly at Charlie. 'You need an awesome imagination to be a good liar. Did you know that?'

I give her a little smile.

After only a few minutes, Charlie takes his mug of

tea and sits out on the step for a smoke, rather than be around us.

Soon as he's gone, I feel some of the tension lift from my neck and shoulders.

'Why is he always round here?' Fallon says. 'He's not your mum's boyfriend, is he?'

'No!' I pull a face at the thought of it. 'He's *Augustine's* boyfriend, and I suppose because she's around here a lot helping Mum, he just tags along.'

'I don't like him.' Fallon's voice drops to a whisper. 'There's something . . . I don't know, *shifty* about him. Was he close to Sam?'

'No, Sam couldn't stand him. He doesn't like us, either . . . but I can't imagine he's done anything to hurt Sam. Besides, the police have questioned him and he bragged they had nothing on him.'

'Best to keep an open mind until we've done our own investigation and know all the details,' Fallon remarks. 'Shame you got stuck with that prat while your dad's inside, though.'

We both burst out laughing. It feels like releasing a blast of burning steam from my lungs.

'Can you stay a bit longer?'

'I was planning to,' she says slowly. 'Unless that's a hint for me to sod off?'

'N-no!' I stammer. 'I only said that because . . . well, you know.'

'Man, you don't half like talking in riddles.'

I take a breath and try to put the words in the right order. 'I thought you might not want to get to know me once you found out my dad is in the nick and, you know –' I sweep my hand around the room – 'we've got no money for stuff.'

'Why would I care about *that*?' She shrugs, looking genuinely perplexed. 'Dad's only a yoga teacher, so money's tight for us too – we don't go for dinner at the Ritz, you know. That's why we're using the food bank for a couple of weeks, to give Dad a chance to get his classes up and running.'

'Yeah, I know, but people around here look down on you if you go there. Some people would rather starve than be seen *scrounging*, as they put it.'

'More fool them, then,' Fallon says airily. 'Nothing wrong in accepting a bit of help when you need it, is there? We've moved around a bit and used food banks before. When Dad gets some regular money, we always take a big bag of food donations in. Paying it forward, you know? That way, everyone gets to help each other.'

'That sounds fair,' I say.

'And as for *your* dad being in prison,' Fallon continues. 'It's you I'm hanging around with, right? Not your old man.'

'But . . . he's my dad. It feels like the prison thing sort

154

of rubs off on the rest of us. People seem to think that Dad going down is a reflection on me, Mum and Sam too. People spread all kinds of horrible rumours about Dad when he was arrested. I'm certain Charlie had something to do with that.'

One night, after Dad was arrested, Mum had gone to the pub with Augustine to drown her sorrows. That's when Augustine had first introduced her to Charlie.

The next morning, we woke up to graffiti on the front door. A couple of days later, a half-brick came sailing through the window from a moving car.

Sam had been playing with his cars in the living room at the time and he'd got tiny shards of broken glass in his hair.

Sylvester told us that a rumour had come out of nowhere. People on the street were saying that Dad had robbed old people's houses all around the estate. There had been a spate of burglaries at that time, but it was totally untrue that Dad had had anything to do with that. He'd never do such a thing.

Mum had drafted a letter to say so and had pushed it through people's letterboxes.

But there had been a bad reaction from some of our neighbours and, suddenly, some of them didn't want us on the street any more.

'Only an idiot like Charlie would think up stuff like

that about your dad and, like I say, there's something off about him,' Fallon says. 'Your dad's mistakes are nothing to do with you, though, are they?'

'No,' I say. 'In fact, I still don't know the full story about why he got sent to prison.'

'That's not on. I mean, I think you have a right to know.' Fallon sits up a bit straighter. 'What *do* you know about it?'

'Literally nothing. Just that Dad was made redundant from his job as a joiner and got involved with a business partner. That's when everything started to go wrong. I remember Dad being excited about the new opportunity, but then in a flash everything changed. Mum said he'd been really secretive, even with her.'

'Hmm. Well, if you were interested in finding out what happened for yourself, then visiting your dad would be a good start.'

'I'm more interested in finding Sam and I hoped Dad might have some ideas. I don't know . . . it's just so frustrating.'

'He'll have heard all about it,' Fallon points out. 'It must be awful, stuck inside when your son is missing.'

'Dad will have nobody to tell him what's really happening, just the official police facts, the bare minimum they have to tell him, probably, and the lies that the press are printing.'

I scratch at my forearms.

We look at each other, and Fallon raises an eyebrow.

'I don't know why they tell lies – it's probably to sell more newspapers,' she says. 'But facing the truth is what's going to find Sam, however hard that might be. There's no room for fairytales.'

DAY THREE

30

I wake up early after a restless night and I creep downstairs so as not to disturb Mum.

Thanks to my trip to the food bank yesterday, there's toast and jam for breakfast. We haven't any butter, but I don't care about that.

I take breakfast into the living room and see that someone has pushed an early edition of the local newspaper through the letterbox. There are one or two journalists outside the gate already and I wonder if it's them.

I take a bite of toast and unfold the paper to read the front page. When I see the headline, I stop chewing and the bread feels like mangled cardboard on my tongue.

Wednesday 25 July

NOTTINGHAM POST

MOTHER OF MISSING LOCAL BOY TOOK OVERDOSE

NOTTINGHAM POST

It has emerged that shortly after her husband's incarceration, Lorraine Clayton, mother of missing 8-year-old local boy Samuel Clayton, took an overdose of prescription drugs.

Speaking outside the family home, Mrs Clayton's friend and neighbour Charles Court told the *Post* about the harrowing incident, which happened shortly after her husband was sentenced.

'It was a terrible time. Lorraine's husband left her penniless and destitute with two young sons. It was left to me and my partner to keep the family together when she was rushed into hospital. Thank God I caught her in time.'

Mr Court explained how he'd found Mrs Clayton unconscious just before the boys arrived home from school.

Mr Court went on to say, 'I think the world of those lads and we've tried our best to protect them and Lorraine after they were cruelly abandoned by their father. Now Sam's gone missing, our world has fallen apart.'

Mr Court has himself been interviewed by detectives, but released without further charge.

'It's easy to blame those who care the most when something like this happens, but I'd lay down my life for those boys,' Mr Court added, close to tears. 'Life's hard for Lorraine at the moment, and we're all worried sick about Sam.'

Earlier, neighbours had told the *Post* that before Sam's disappearance, he was often left in the sole care of his older brother, Ed, for long periods of time.

Officers are expected to visit HMP Nottingham to speak to Philip Clayton, Samuel's father, who is currently serving his third year of a ten-year sentence.

Sam Clayton went missing late on Sunday afternoon while visiting Bulwell Hall Park with his 14-year-old brother. Edward Clayton fell from play equipment and sustained a head injury. He still has no memory of the incident.

Police say they have an ongoing enquiry and are confident progress will be made.

The child has now been missing for over 48 hours.

Anyone who has any further information about Sam's disappearance should contact Nottinghamshire Police Force confidentially.

I push the paper to one side so I don't have to look at it any more. They've made it sound as if Mum took those tablets on purpose.

What effect is this going to have when she sees Charlie's betrayal . . . his lies, telling the papers a made-up story about Mum's illness and hospital visit?

I hate even thinking about that day, but, thanks to Charlie, I can't stop the memory from coming.

When Mum had been discharged from hospital and was feeling a little better, she sat both me and Sam down.

'It was an accident,' she said. 'Don't let anyone tell you otherwise. I'm not feeling well and I'm confused and forgetful. That's all it was. I took the pills twice and, because they're strong, I knocked myself out.'

On the day it happened, it'd been me who'd found

163

Mum. I ran straight across the road to get Augustine. Charlie had been at the pub, and Mum had already been taken to hospital when he came home.

My whole body itches, like my skin is trying to peel away from my flesh.

Thanks to Charlie, they're implying that it was Mum's fault that Sam went missing.

I'm so mad at Charlie, but I'm just as angry with myself.

I sit there for ages just running everything through my mind.

I make Mum a cup of tea and take it upstairs, but she's still asleep, so I don't wake her up. There is a foil strip of tablets on the floor next to the bed. I recognize them as the same little blue ones she used to take when she was going through her *bad time*. The same ones that made her slur her words and sleep all day.

She opens her eyes.

'Morning, Ed. Any news?'

I shake my head and look at the floor.

A churning feeling starts up in my stomach. I don't tell her about the newspaper article.

I just watch her until she falls asleep again.

'Where are you, Sam?' I whisper.

This is the kind of situation where the adults should

be in control. But in this house all the adults do is make a mess of everything.

I just want my brother back.

I can't hear a sound in the house. There are no well-wishers here, Augustine and Charlie haven't come over yet, and now Jill and the detectives are staying away unless they have something they need to say face to face to Mum.

The police are still calling at the house two or three times a day to update Mum, but unless there's big news Charlie says they have to stay at the door with all the flashing cameras in the background.

'I'll teach them to try to humiliate me,' he says, like that's all that matters.

Just as the silence seems to ring in my ears, I hear a door open and a pinched little cough from in the kitchen, like steam flicking up a saucepan lid. Augustine. She's always been here for me, Sam and Mum.

'Mum has gone back to sleep,' I tell her. 'Charlie has been talking to the newspapers. He's said some things that aren't true, and Mum will—'

'Don't worry, love. I'll sort it all out. He's a flaming idiot.' She puts her arm round me.

If she thinks Charlie is such an idiot, then why is she with him? I feel like bursting into tears and burying my head in her shoulder, but instead I move away.

'I just wish there was something I could do,' I say.

'The police are doing everything they can,' Augustine says in her calming voice. 'And they'll find Sam and he'll be fine. I just know it.'

She's saying it just to make me feel better. How can anyone be sure Sam is OK until we find him?

'Where can he be, though?' I sigh. 'I'm scared Mum will get really anxious when she sees that newspaper article.'

'I'll sit with her and explain,' Augustine says. 'I know it's tough, but try not to worry. Everything will come good in the end.'

I'm not a little kid and this is not a story in a book. But she means well.

'I could make you a cup of tea,' I say.

'Lovely, thanks, Ed.' She smiles. 'One sugar, please.'

I pad quietly downstairs to the kitchen, relieved someone else is here to help with Mum. It's really hard to know what to say or do when Mum gets down because nothing seems to make it any better.

I wash last night's dishes in the sink without soap because we've run out again, and then I remember there's no milk for Augustine's tea. I'll still make it, without. When I open the sugar canister, it's completely empty apart from a few rock-hard grains on the sides.

I root around in the drawer, looking for one of the little cafe sachets of sugar that Mum brings home in her handbag.

A sudden flare of temper at the hopelessness of everything has me pulling the whole thing out and upending it on the counter. I find a tiny packet of sugar and something else catches my eye too.

Something that must have been tucked at the back of the drawer for a long time.

31

I push the papers deep in my back pocket and take Augustine's tea up.

'I'm going next door for a bit to see Fallon,' I say, 'if that's OK?'

'Course it is, love,' Augustine says, looking down at her black tea. 'Don't tell her too much about what's happening, though, eh?'

I nod and walk back downstairs, wondering what Augustine means. Nothing *is* happening, so far as I can tell.

I tap on the back door and Neil's voice calls out. 'Come in!'

I step inside and see he's making bacon and mushroom sandwiches. My mouth starts to water.

'Go through, Ed,' he says. 'Fallon's in the front room. Fancy a bit of breakfast?'

'It's OK, thanks. I've just had a fry-up.'

I could kick myself for turning it down, but you just get used to your belly rumbling after a while.

The thing that bothers you the most about being poor is not that there are no big fancy meals to eat. It's the little things, like if you feel like a bag of crisps or something, you can't just go to the cupboard and get one.

There are no such things as snacks or treats, and I can't remember the last time we had pizza. Meals just consist of stuff that fills you up, like white bread and baked beans.

Neil tips his head to one side and looks at me like Fallon does.

'Sure about that? There's plenty to go round. I did a yoga class for the vegan group at the community centre and they gave me food in payment.'

Hang on . . . the *vegan* group gave him bacon? Weird. I take a deep breath.

'Actually, yeah, thanks, I will. I didn't want to put you to any trouble, but I'm starving.'

'Cool.' He smiles to himself and prods at the bacon sizzling in the pan with a wooden spoon.

I find Fallon in the front room.

'Ed!' Fallon puts down her book and sits up straight. As usual, she's dressed in layers of mismatched floral clothing, worn with purple leggings. 'How's things. Any news?'

'Nah.' I sit down heavily on the settee. It's covered in multi-coloured throws with sequins and tassels on them. 'No news. But . . . I found something, in the drawer at home.'

I lean forward and pull out the wedge of papers from my back pocket.

Fallon's eyes widen and she hops over to sit next to me, helping me straighten them out.

'These are visiting orders from the prison,' I say. 'Dad has sent them regularly every few weeks, obviously hoping Mum will bring me and Sam to see him.'

'But she told you your dad didn't want anyone to visit, right?'

'Right. And that's what I believed until now. But all this time Dad must've felt really lonely and tried to see us.' My voice cracks and I cough to try to cover it up. 'He must think I don't care about him.'

'Don't be daft.' Fallon shakes her head. 'I bet he'll have guessed what's happened. You must have missed him so much all this time.'

I nod, not trusting myself to speak without bursting into tears.

'I can't imagine how you coped when your dad first went to prison.'

I'd always tried not to think about it, but Fallon mentioning it seems to loosen up the locked memories.

'When Dad first went away, it honestly felt like a big empty space opened up inside me. Nobody knew it was there but me, and it's still there, but I suppose I've just got used to it.'

Fallon nods. 'I think a lot of people have empty spaces inside like that . . . caused by stuff that's happened to them. Sometimes people cover it up with anger or spite.'

'Or lies,' I say softly.

'When really they're just sad.' Fallon gives me a small smile.

'The first year that Dad was away, I used to save up bits of change until I had enough for the bus fare to Perry Road in Nottingham.'

'But you couldn't visit him?'

I shake my head. 'I'd stand outside the prison walls, staring at the grey concrete, imagining what Dad might be doing in there. Just being nearer to him made me feel less alone.'

'That's really sad,' Fallon whispers.

'Yeah. I used to stand in the same spot, but it was only after a few times doing it that I saw the tree. A spindly thing that someone had propped up against a stick because it wasn't strong enough to support itself.'

I remember the pavement was grey, cracked concrete, the wall of the prison was grey concrete, the road was black asphalt, and then there was this brown and green tree . . . the only living thing on the street.

'I don't know why, but I felt better, knowing the tree was there, day and night. Sounds really stupid, but somehow it made me believe that Dad would be OK.'

'I can understand that,' Fallon says. 'Trees are living things.'

'Imran, my mate, he lent me his phone to take a photo. We printed it out at school and that single time I visited

Dad, I told him about the tree and gave him the picture.'

Dad laughed, and then a few weeks later he wrote to me and said he'd put the photo up on his cell wall.

'You and your dad, you were close, right?' Fallon asks gently.

I nod. 'We used to do lots of stuff together: go down the canal; he'd take me and Sam to the park. And he used to love coming to watch me play football for the school team.' I realize it's a long time since I've thought about this stuff.

'Do you still play?' Neil asks, carrying plates of bacon sandwiches in.

'Not any more,' I say, thanking him as I take a plate.

'Why's that, then?' Neil sits in the chair and takes a big bite of his sandwich.

'Dunno, really. I think it was seeing all the other dads there, at the sidelines. It made me miss Dad even more and I just kind of stopped playing.'

It's also because of Aidan and his gang, but I don't tell Neil that.

'Can I tell Dad?' Fallon says. 'About what you've found?'

I nod and she tells him about the visiting orders and how after visiting Dad, Mum had then told me Dad didn't want to see me any more.

'That's bang out of order.' Neil frowns. 'Can I see the orders?'

He takes them from me and scans through them.

'He only sent the last one a month ago.' Neil shakes his head. 'It's wrong, not letting you see him. Very wrong.'

'Can you keep these here for me?' I ask them. 'I'm going to speak to Jill, the police family liaison officer. I've already spoken to her about Dad and she's going to see what she can do.'

'Course, no problem,' Neil says, and Fallon nods. 'And you can tell Jill that I'm happy to go with you if you need adult accompaniment.'

To my horror, my eyes fill up and then brim over. I turn away and wipe my face with the back of my hand.

'Thanks, Neil,' I say, looking at the floor.

'Come on, then. Get those sandwiches down you!'

I grin and take a bite. It tastes gorgeous . . . of bacon, as I'd expected. But, somehow, it doesn't feel like bacon when I chew it.

'Your face!' Fallon bursts out laughing.

'Enjoying it, Ed?' Neil grins.

'Yes, it's lovely. Thank you.' I'm careful to mind my manners. It's really kind of Neil to make me breakfast.

'We call it *fakeon*, not bacon,' Neil explains. 'We're vegans, so we don't eat any animal products. You can leave it if you don't like it, though. I won't be offended.'

'It's lovely,' I say, and I mean it. 'Thanks.'

For the first time since Sam went missing, I do feel properly hungry.

Maybe it's hope making me feel better. That, finally, I might get to see my dad.

32

After breakfast, Fallon and I tidy up the kitchen while Neil gets ready for his morning yoga class.

We've both agreed to start our own investigations this morning.

'Let's go to the park and your den,' Fallon suggests. 'That's kind of starting from the beginning.'

It's just the sort of day that me and Sam might take ourselves off down to Bulwell Hall Park with his jam jar and net. A little sunshine, not much wind . . . perfect fishing weather.

'We can go down to the big pond first,' I tell Fallon. 'If we're lucky, it'll be quiet down there.'

But when we reach the top of the hill, Barker's Wood is right next to us. The tall trees wave and rustle in the breeze, seeming to beckon us in, and I feel the pull of the den.

The perfect place to hide out for a while, away from everything.

'I brought the police here,' I explain to Fallon. 'There was no sign of Sam then, but what if he's made his way back from wherever he was . . . ? What if he's hiding there now?'

'There's only one way to find out.' Fallon nods. 'Let's take a look before we go down to the park.'

We stop walking and look around. Once we're satisfied there is nobody watching, I slip into the trees and Fallon follows.

'Gosh, it's so quiet in here,' Fallon murmurs, tipping her head back to stare up at the tops of the enormous trees. 'It's beautiful.'

I allow myself to be swallowed up by the gloominess. I agree with Fallon: the silence is comforting.

We begin to move deftly through the trees, the only sound the crunch of the twigs and branches beneath our feet.

The wood feels like my friend, my confidante. I'm tempted to say all the stuff that's bothering me out loud, let it free among the cool leaves that brush against my hands and face, but Fallon will think I've lost it, so I stay silent.

I head towards the den, my shoulders relaxing a little more with each step. I don't know why it hasn't occurred to me to come here again before now. It's a place I feel close to Sam; a place he loves as much as I do.

I take a sharp left turn from the narrow path just before the tree stump, making sure as always that there is no gap in the branches. I hear Fallon's footfall right behind me.

We battle through the tangle of greenery until I reach the den's 'curtain', and then I slip silently through into Sam's and my little oasis.

There's a tangled yellow 'Police Line: Do Not Cross' banner discarded on the floor like a poisonous snake.

'Ooh!' Fallon exclaims when she steps in behind me. 'This is really cool!'

I see immediately that one of the deckchairs is unfolded and placed in the centre of the den. A creeping sense of unease begins to prickle at the base of my spine.

'Something's not right,' I whisper, and put out an arm to stop Fallon walking in any further.

'Why, what's wrong?'

'Before we leave the den, we always make a point of folding up the chairs and tucking them towards the back out of the way of any spots of rain that might sneak through our branch canopy,' I say. 'When I came here with the police, I didn't get to see the den, so not sure when it happened, but now . . . that chair's been moved.'

A branch cracks behind me and I whip my head round.

'Sorry.' Fallon bites her lip. 'Just me, shifting about.'

I take a few more steps inside and look around for any signs of disturbance, but there doesn't seem to be anything else out of place.

I remember that I'd left the police in the den and waited down the path with Augustine. Maybe one of the policemen moved the chair out for some reason.

I sit down on the chair and close my eyes. Last time

I was in the den, I had my brother with me. Yes, he was upset and his clothes were wet, but he was here. Safe and sound.

'Ed, are you OK?' Fallon whispers.

'Yeah, just thinking.' Something about the silence of the wood makes me whisper too.

I shift in my seat and look down at the corner where Sam always used to put his collections of funny-shaped twigs and stones. And then I remember.

I spring off the chair and begin scrabbling around in the leaves.

'What's wrong?' Fallon hisses. 'What have you found?'

'Nothing yet, but I remembered . . . Sam's treasures are down here somewhere.' My fingers hit a hard surface and I pull out an old tin box.

'Cute!' Fallon says.

'He kept all his precious bits in here, acorns and pressed flowers.'

Her grin fades. 'Poor Sam.'

I force the wonky lid open and look inside. The tin is empty apart from a folded piece of white paper and a pen.

I pick it up, unfold it and hold it up to the scant light filtering through the canopy. It's covered in red scrawl that I can't quite read properly in the shadowy light.

'What is it?' Fallon steps closer.

'There's something written on here. I need light.'

'Here, use this.' Fallon presses a button on her phone

and a torch beam emits from it.

Fallon flattens out the paper on the seat and I shine the torchlight on to it while I read Sam's misspelled, messy handwriting out loud.

Ed, I am OK Carnt say were I am in caSe someone Reeds this will tell You more Soon
DON'T TELL ANYONE

Love Sam x

I feel like throwing up and laughing all at once.

'Is this some kind of a sick joke?' Fallon's hand flies over her mouth.

'I'm certain Sam has left this here for me to find,' I say.

'What if it's just a sick trick? Someone put it there to make you think Sam wrote it?'

I shake my head. 'It's definitely Sam's handwriting, and nobody else but me and him know this tin even exists. I reckon he left the chair out so I'd see immediately someone had been here. We were always really strict about putting everything away before we left the den.'

'But if Sam has been able to come here after he'd supposedly gone missing, does that mean he's run away? He's done it before.'

'I don't think he's run away on his own.' I frown,

179

looking back at the tin. 'He's taken all his precious bits with him and left the note . . . He can't come home for some reason, but he wanted me to find his message.'

'*Can't say where I am in case someone reads this,*' Fallon continues.

'Who does he mean by "someone"?' I think aloud. 'Is someone holding Sam against his will?'

'If someone's abducted him, then why would they bring him back here? Surely they wouldn't have let him write a note!'

'I know, and if he was back in the den, wouldn't Sam have been able to escape?'

'None of it makes sense,' Fallon says.

She's right – it doesn't make sense. But for once I push my over-thinking aside and allow my gut feelings to surface instead.

'I believe Sam wrote this note and left it for only me to find. He must have had time to take his things out of the tin and write the note . . . It's a mystery, but if it's true it means Sam must be OK, like he says in the message.'

'What now?' Fallon's eyes are wide.

'I'll have to tell the police,' I say. 'I've no choice.'

If someone is keeping Sam against his will, then they need to know about it.

But then my eyes settle again on the capital letters that Sam has written so boldly and even underlined. *Don't tell anyone.*

'What if Sam is really OK? If I go to the police, then the person who has him will know he left a note. They might get really angry and . . . well, anything could happen.' I shake my head in confusion.

Fallon reads the note again, line by line.

'*Ed, I am OK*. Well, that's fairly straightforward. Sam wants to let you know he is OK,' Fallon remarks. 'He's eight years old. He probably *is* OK. Younger kids say it like it is.'

I turn the note over and pick up the pen.

Sam, you MUST tell me where you are. We are worried and upset. Ed x

I fold up the note and shut it back inside the tin. 'Just in case he comes back here,' I say.

'It's very confusing,' Fallon says as I rebury it under the leaves. 'But there's one thing we can say now.'

I look at her, puzzled.

'We've only just started our own investigation and we've already made progress, which is more than the police can say.'

33

We both stumble out of the woods in a bit of a daze.

'I'm going to try and speak to Mum first,' I tell Fallon when we climb back into my garden. 'When Charlie and Augustine aren't there.'

I don't want Augustine sharing this with Charlie in case he runs to the papers again.

Fallon nods. 'OK, come round later, if you can.'

When I get home, the house is quiet.

Mum sits in her chair in the living room, staring out of the window at the dull sky. She used to do this for hours on end when Dad first went to prison; she couldn't even sleep. That's why the doctor gave her the little blue tablets in the first place.

'You OK, Mum?'

She doesn't look at me, doesn't say anything.

I sit on the settee opposite her and study her face. Her skin has taken on a papery translucence as if it is somehow thinner. Her eyes are hard, dark hollows that stay wide open and hardly blink at all.

'Where's Augustine?' I ask.

'She had to go, had a community meeting,' Mum says vaguely.

'And Charlie?'

Mum stays quiet.

'Are you hungry?' I say, suddenly desperate to make her feel better. 'I could heat up a tin of soup.'

'Can't you just be quiet?' she snaps, and then her eyes fill up. 'I'm sorry, Ed. I just . . . I just miss our Sam so much.'

I press my fingers into the thin seat cushion beneath me and take a deep breath.

'Mum, there's something I need to tell you, but it's really, really important you don't tell anyone else. Not Charlie, not even Augustine.'

Her head jerks up. 'What is it?' she whispers. 'Have you remembered what happened that day?'

'No, but Sam is OK.' I smile, reaching for her hand. 'He wrote me a note, hid it in our den so I'd find it.'

Her eyes widen in disbelief.

'He's coming home soon, Mum. I don't know who's got him, but he's going to be OK and—'

'Stop it!' Mum screams the words so loud I jump up out of my seat. 'How could you lie to me at a time like this?'

'Mum, I swear . . . it's true!'

She looks at me a moment longer, then clamps her hand across her mouth and turns to the window again. Her shoulders sag, like her whole body is folding inwards, as she begins to sob.

'I don't want to upset you, Mum, but I'm telling the truth. Sam left me a note, but begged me not to tell anyone.'

'Where is it, then, this note?'

'I left it there, hidden under some leaves. I wrote him a message back just in case he comes to the den again,' I say. I get up and sit on the arm of her chair. 'I'm telling the truth, Mum. I swear.'

She shakes her head, but doesn't say anything.

After a while, her crying becomes soft and quiet and hardly there. And she doesn't pull away when I rest my hand on hers.

We stay like that until the scant light fills with plum and indigo shades that slowly fade from the sky.

But no more words are spoken.

I go upstairs to my room and lie on my bed.

Tiredness is starting to catch up with me again. But my head is full of questions, even more now I've found that note.

I grab my homework diary from the side of the bed and try to put my thoughts down in some logical order.

Q: Do I believe Sam wrote the note?

A: *Yes. It's definitely his handwriting.*

Q: Do I believe Sam has run away on his own?

A: *No. I don't believe this because he had no reason to run away, and even if he did, he would hide out in the den*

until he got cold and then come home. He has obviously
visited the den, but then gone away somewhere else.

Q: Do I think Sam has been abducted?

A: *Yes.*

Q: Do I think someone has forced Sam to write the
note to pretend he is OK when he isn't?

A: *No. If someone had forced Sam to write the note,*
he'd have left it out in full view. He wouldn't have hidden
the note in the tin and then buried it. He wanted to send
me a secret note without anyone knowing.

I read back through what I've written and sigh.

It still makes no sense.

Later, I decide to pop across the road to Augustine's to talk
to her about Mum.

There is still no sign of Charlie, but that's a good thing.
I know I'll be back again before Mum even notices I'm
out.

Augustine and Mum were good friends before, but
Sam's disappearance has brought them even closer
together.

Looking at Augustine's windows, it's hard to tell if
anyone is home, but as I get closer I spot a light on in
the back kitchen. I can partly see Augustine. Her back is
facing the window and her hands are moving in front of
her, as if she's talking to someone.

I think about turning round and going back home. I

shouldn't really interrupt her if she has a visitor. But then I decide that, even if I don't go inside, I can just ask her to keep a closer eye on Mum in the next couple of days.

The concrete step at Augustine's front door is covered with a thin layer of slippery moss that looks just like wet green icing. I stand there and raise my fist to knock at the door.

My heart is walloping away again. I can't decide whether to tell Augustine about Sam's note. She's been so good to us. But Mum called me a liar, and what if Augustine thinks the same?

Finding Sam's note has made me want to see Dad more than ever. He'll know what to do for the best. I'm sick and tired of being surrounded by adults who are good at telling me what to do, where to go and what I should and shouldn't say, but who are not so good themselves at making any progress in finding my brother.

I knock at the door and peer through the big pane of opaque, patterned glass.

No answer.

I knock again, harder this time.

There's no answer.

I knock on the wood first, then on the glass, making it rattle slightly.

I press my face right up close and try to see through it. The pattern on the glass distorts everything, but I can just about make out the light and a few blurred shapes

186

beyond. Nothing that looks like a person, nothing that's moving.

I turn and walk away. When I get back to our gate and close it behind me, I look over there one last time.

I swear the living-room curtain moves on one side, just a touch. I dash behind a hedge and watch. A face appears . . . Whiskers and rough skin, a man's head turning this way and that, but then his eyes focus on our house across the road.

I suddenly feel dizzy and crouch down so I don't lose my balance. The pavement fades away and a picture flashes in my mind – of being outside my gate and seeing that face watching our house . . . could this be who I meant when I told Imran I thought someone was monitoring us?

34

'It's driving me crazy,' I tell Fallon when I go round to her house after Augustine's. 'How could Sam escape long enough to leave a note and then be captured again . . . ? It doesn't make any sense.'

'Either Sam is tricking everyone by pretending someone has taken him, or a big piece of the jigsaw is missing that's stopping us making sense of it.'

I nod. I can feel something building inside me . . . a sort of pressure.

'So, are you going to tell the police, or not?'

I shake my head. 'I don't know. Did you tell your dad?'

'No. He's still taking classes.' She hesitates. 'And I didn't know if you'd want me to.'

'I told Mum.' A buzz starts up in my head. 'But she didn't believe me, anyway.'

Fallon presses her lips together.

'What is it?' I ask her.

'Well, I was just thinking . . . The police are doing everything they can, but they don't know about Sam's note. Do you think you have a responsibility to tell them? I mean—'

'It's not that easy. If Mum thinks I'm lying, then the

police will too. Charlie keeps telling them and the press that I can't be trusted. Sam's note specifically said to tell nobody. I can't afford to put him in danger. And there's something else . . . '

Fallon waits. 'Go on.'

'Well, I can't help thinking, what if some crank has left the note, you know, to send us off down the wrong track? You hear about that sort of thing happening in cases, don't you? People who have nothing to do with the investigation trying to bring attention to themselves.'

'Hmm, I suppose it's possible. But what if it's genuine and the police find out that you've withheld information . . . what then?'

'I think I probably will have to tell the police.' I sigh. 'But not just yet. Are you doing anything right now?'

'Nope.'

'Come back to mine, then,' I say. 'We can search through Sam's things while Charlie is out and Mum's in bed.'

Back at my house, we creep upstairs and I close my bedroom door behind us.

'That's Sam's bed,' I say sadly.

Fallon sits on the edge of it and bends double to look under it.

'There's a big plastic box under here,' she says.

'They're just his toy cars.'

We check under the mattress, inside his pillowcase.

Fallon takes Sam's few books from his shelf and flicks through them.

'I haven't a clue what I'm looking for.' She sighs.

I go to Sam's side of the wardrobe. He hasn't got many clothes, but I search through all the pockets anyway. Then I check through the games he keeps on the wardrobe floor.

Fallon crouches down and reaches for the box under the bed.

I sit and watch as she takes out the cars separately and checks them over. I feel heavy and tired, like I'm filled to the brim with hopelessness.

Fallon takes out a large American Mustang.

'That's his favourite car,' I tell her, my voice flat. 'Sam could play for hours with it.'

Fallon flips a switch and the boot flips open. 'What's this?' she whispers.

She pulls out a piece of white paper, folded up so it fits exactly into the hidden space.

'You open it, Ed.' She hands it to me.

My hands are shaking a little as I quickly open it up.

'It's a picture he's drawn!' Fallon studies it.

My heart sinks. I'd really thought it might be another note, another clue.

'We might as well go downstairs,' I say. 'It might be best to—'

'Ed, wait,' Fallon says, still staring at the coloured picture. 'Look at this. Sam's drawn himself next to you.

I think that must be Charlie and your mum. And look –'
she points a finger – 'is that Augustine, holding a box?'

'Looks like it,' I say. 'What does that say?' I squint at
the tiny writing on the box. 'S – E – E – K – R – I – T.'

'What does that mean?' Fallon frowns.

'I think it's SECRET,' I say excitedly. 'It's secret, spelled
wrong.'

35

We both start at raised voices downstairs.

I tell Fallon to go out the front, that I'll see her in her backyard in half an hour, and I creep across the landing, slipping down each stair, avoiding every one that creaks, and stand outside the kitchen door. Through the slender opening, I can see Mum and Charlie are in there.

'What's wrong with you, Lorraine?' Charlie grumbles. 'Augustine has gone crazy at me, thanks to you. Anyone else would be pleased that they're in a national newspaper.'

I see Mum stop whatever it is she's doing over the other side of the kitchen and turn round to glare at him. She must've seen that latest article about her accidental overdose, after all.

'I don't want to do any press interviews,' she says. 'And I don't want you inviting any more neighbours round for drinks like it's a non-stop party. Sam has gone missing. Can you get that into your thick skull? That's no reason to be celebrating.'

'You've got some funny ideas,' Charlie snaps back. 'Everybody knows it pays to keep the press and the locals onside. Everybody already thinks you're a bad mother, a scrounger who neglects your kids. You need to keep the interest going by showing them your human side.'

'Interest? It's my son we're talking about here, Charlie. You don't get any more human than wanting your missing son back home.'

'That's just it. Sam is *your* son, Lorraine, not theirs. They forget all too quickly, get on with chasing the next story. The police will soon get fed up of keeping half the force on this case. They're already asking questions about how often Sam goes out on his own. I know it's awful, but it's true.'

'And to keep their interest I've got to turn a blind eye to the newspapers digging up my own personal history?' A tear rolls down Mum's cheek. 'That article talks about my depression and about Phil being in prison.'

Charlie sighs. 'Articles like this one keep people thinking about the case. We have to feed them bits of information to keep them coming back, keep them wanting to find Sam. You shouldn't take it personally.'

Mum looks at him and shakes her head in disgust.

'It was *you*. The *Post* got their story about me having depression from you.'

He shrugs.

'I just told the reporter you'd been doing well after a period of being low, and then she wanted to know what was wrong with you back then. They have to have something juicy to keep selling newspapers, love. Don't you realize that?'

'You promised not to say anything to anyone about it.' Mum wipes her eyes with the back of her hand. 'I didn't even know you back then. It was a rotten thing to do.'

Mum has always blindly put her faith in Charlie. Trusted him as much as Augustine. I've never understood it.

'I didn't promise anything.' Charlie gives a cruel laugh. 'Stop being so paranoid. It seems to me you're more worried about keeping your own reputation intact than finding out where your son is.'

I feel my blood gushing and bubbling hot in my veins. But I keep quiet.

'Never!' Mum cries out. 'But I explained to you that it was private and I don't want people judging me. I don't want people around here saying our Sam wasn't properly looked after because I'm not capable. If I was disabled or had a physical illness, they'd be more understanding. If you're unwell in your mind, some folks think you're just putting it on.'

'Mark my words, a good sob story will help find Sam,' Charlie remarks. 'The media love it.'

There is a pause during which I suddenly realize I am breathing far too loudly as I imagine summoning superhuman strength and picking Charlie up. I could hold him high above my head while he's screaming for mercy, before throwing him uber fast, away from us forever.

The kitchen door flies open and Charlie grabs my sleeve as I try to take off.

'You sly little dog. Listening to other people's conversations that are nothing to do with you now?'

'Get off me!' I twist and turn until he loosens his grip. 'You're making everything worse, upsetting Mum like this.'

'Charlie, leave him alone,' Mum says wearily.

'Leave him alone?' he rants, shaking me like a ragdoll. 'We wouldn't be in this bloody mess if it wasn't for *him*.'

'When my dad hears what you've been up to, he'll sucker punch you when he gets out.'

Charlie laughs, shakes his head.

'Daydreaming again.' He rolls his eyes at Mum.

I feel a rage uncurling inside me, but it's aimed at Mum, not useless Charlie.

'I've got a right to see my dad,' I shout at Mum. 'He's got a right to know what's happening with Sam from us, not just strangers.'

The smile disappears from Charlie's face, and Mum holds on to the worktop as if she feels suddenly weak.

'Leave it, Ed,' Mum whispers, her face pale.

'No! I won't leave it,' I yell. 'Has anyone thought about speaking to Dad about all this? Sam is his son too, you know. He's stuck in prison, probably reading the newspapers and wondering what's happened. Someone should—'

Charlie grabs me round the throat and pushes his pockmarked face into mine.

'Been ferreting around in the bins, have you?'

'What?'

'You should be worrying more about your poor mother than that criminal.'

'I want to know what happened, why Dad got sent down.' I look over Charlie's shoulder, trying to appeal directly to Mum. 'I've got a right to know.'

'I won't tell you again.' He bares his crooked nicotine-stained teeth and presses his face even closer to mine. 'Just leave it. You're upsetting your mother, you little swine.'

I turn away from his stale breath and look over at Mum again, pleading silently with her, but she doesn't say anything.

She just looks at me with those dull, lifeless eyes and slowly shakes her head.

36

Upstairs, I wait until I hear Charlie leave the house and then open my door, just in time to see Mum closing her own bedroom door.

'Mum, can we talk?'

'Not now,' she says from behind the door. 'I'm too tired, Ed.'

'I'd really like to go and visit Dad . . . He might be able to help us in some way. He might be able to help us find Sam.'

'Leave it, Ed. I just can't face it today.'

I wait until I hear Mum's bedsprings groan as she lies down, then I go downstairs and straight out to the wheelie bin.

Charlie's words have been echoing in my ears ever since he uttered them earlier: *Been ferreting around in the bins, have you?* I knew then that there must be something in there he doesn't want me to see.

I open the bin lid and brace myself to be immersed in a cloud of stink, but it's not too bad. Mum hasn't been cooking and Augustine is a big fan of sandwiches.

A load of paperwork has been tossed in the bottom. I lie the bin on its side and scoop out most of the papers. It's mainly junk mail, but I spot the corner of a plain white envelope and pull it out.

The front has been inked with some kind of official stamp. I can decipher 'H.M.P.', and that's about it. My breath catches in my throat. This looks like a letter from prison.

I slip the envelope in the waistband of my jeans and make sure I clear up every last piece of paper before setting the bin straight. I go back inside and wash my hands at the kitchen sink and then I go and sit in what used to be Dad's chair and read the letter.

It's a single sheet from H.M.P. Nottingham, addressed to Mum.

<u>VISITING ORDER</u>
Prisoner 529103

Philip Clayton has granted you permission to visit.

Please select 3 possible dates and times for your visit below.

You will receive a confirmation email within three working days.

My hands shake as I read the order again and again. This is another order in addition to the ones I found in the kitchen drawer. Dad is trying desperately to see us.

Has Mum already requested a visit to talk to Dad about

Sam, and Charlie has intercepted it? Or has Dad sent the order in the hope she will go to see him . . . and possibly take me with her?

I feel a terrible sense of urgency rip through me when I see it is dated only two days previously. Do these things expire?

After staring in disbelief at the paper for a while longer, I glance at the clock and see I have only five minutes to spare.

I fold the new visiting order neatly and stuff it in my back pocket. Then I leave the house to wait in Fallon's back garden, as planned.

I realize as I get closer that I'm looking forward to seeing her, to spending time with someone who wants to help and who I can trust. With Fallon, I feel I can tell the truth and leave the lies out of it.

'I've got something to show you,' I say urgently when she comes out.

'Do you fancy going to the food-bank cafe?'

I don't really, but we have to talk somewhere, and Charlie could come back at any time.

We go down there and Fallon grabs a table while I get the drinks. I pull my baseball cap down and walk through the busy tables. One or two people look at me, but nobody says anything about Sam going missing.

We sit down.

'I hope you don't mind me suggesting we come here

first,' Fallon says, busily arranging four sugar sachets into a perfect square on the tabletop. 'This is one of the few places I feel you can come without feeling judged. The people who run it accept people as they find them when they walk through the door.'

'I feel comfortable here,' I say. 'And we can plan what we're going to do about Sam's note, but first take a look at this. I rescued it from the bin this morning. Someone – I'm guessing maybe Charlie – threw it away and nobody knows I have it.'

I hand her the new visiting order and watch her eyes widen.

We look at each other.

'I'm so desperate to see Dad, I feel like I'm going to explode,' I say, covering my face with my hands. 'He'll know what to do about Sam's note and whether I should take it to the police.'

'Ed, don't you see – this is amazing, even if you can't visit him yet.'

I let my hands drop away and look at her, not sure what she means.

'Now you have your dad's prisoner number.'

'So?'

'So . . . you can write to him directly!'

I would have been so happy about this even just a week ago, but now . . . Now it's not enough. I need to *see* Dad face to face. I've been kept away from him long enough.

We leave the cafe and turn on to the Main Street.

'Hey, look, it's that boy whose little brother is missing!' someone calls. 'Doesn't look too bothered, does he?'

I spin round and scan the street. Then someone else shouts from the opposite side.

'He's laughing. Can you believe it?'

'Yeah, he reckons he can't remember, but the police think he's lying.'

'Come on.' Fallon grabs my hand and starts to run.

I feel dizzy. There are a lot of people dotted around looking at us, but they're all blurring into one. These are people who I've never seen before shouting at me angrily.

'Running away are you?'

'Where is he, then? You were there!'

'Get a life, you losers!' Fallon yells as we pick up pace.

'Don't listen to them.' She gives me a sideways glance. 'We'll find Sam and then they'll eat their words.'

But my heavy heart tells me we might not find him.

What if the note is a red herring and Sam is in real danger?

Something is bubbling away inside me, and with each new day I can feel it rising up and up. At this moment in time it feels as if it's just about ready to come spilling out.

When I get home, I open the kitchen door and stop dead at the sound of voices. Augustine and Charlie are talking in our living room.

I'm not in the mood for visitors. I'm not in the mood for looking at Charlie's ugly grinning face. I just want to go upstairs and shut my bedroom door, but then something makes me freeze. I hear Dad's name.

'He could be out early with good behaviour,' I hear Charlie grumble. 'Then where will we be?'

'I've told you before – you've got to stop saying this stuff. Leave it to – Who's there?' Augustine calls out.

I curse myself for breathing too hard. Why were they talking about Dad?

I push open the door and get ready to challenge both of them, but as soon as I see Augustine's face I know something is wrong.

'Where's Mum?' I ask faintly.

'They've taken her to the hospital, Ed, but don't panic. She's going to be OK.' Augustine steps closer to me and lays her hand gently on my arm.

'What happened?' I whisper.

'She took a turn for the worse about an hour ago.'

Augustine looks out of the window at the now scant gathering of press at the gate. 'She's finding it difficult to cope, needs a break from that lot.' She jerks her head to the journalists and cameramen.

I squeeze my eyes shut. 'I shouldn't have gone out with Fallon when Mum wasn't feeling well.'

'You weren't to know she'd get worse,' Augustine says. 'She just needs some rest, Ed. And she needs professional help.'

I shake my head and wipe my eyes with the back of my hand.

'They're keeping her in overnight, just to let her have some rest. You know it's the nature of the illness that she goes through these phases.'

Depression . . . anxiety . . . I *hate* them. They take my mum and turn her into someone else.

'I should be there with her,' I say, patting my pockets as if I'll miraculously find some cash.

'No, Ed. She said to tell you to wait until tomorrow. They've sedated her now to give her mind a rest from the trauma.'

'There's something else as well' Charlie mumbles. He doesn't sound like his usual self.

'I'm listening,' I hear myself say. Tendrils of dread squirm around in my stomach.

'The council have threatened to revoke your mum's tenancy on the house.'

'I'm sorry, love,' Augustine says softly.

I shake my head. 'They can't just throw us out of the house . . . with Mum in hospital and Sam still missing. The newspapers would make them look bad.'

'I'm just saying, they *might* do it,' Charlie adds. 'With your mum losing her cleaning job, it's looking bleak. She's already behind with the rent. Maybe they'll just move you, but it'll be to somewhere a lot smaller than this place.'

I listen to his words and they start to fade as my imagination fills in the blanks of how life might be . . .

Crammed into a tiny flat.

With an even emptier fridge.

Unpaid rent.

Mum's health worsening so she can't ever get out of bed.

Is this what rock bottom feels like? When the electric card ran out once, the day before Mum got her cleaning-job money, we just had bread and cold beans to eat. That's how we ended up seeking help from the food bank.

It sounds awful, but it's amazing how good stuff like that can taste when you're hungry.

'Are you listening?' Augustine asks.

'Yes, I heard him,' I say.

'If only we could get some money from somewhere . . .' Charlie's words tail off. 'Do you know of any money, Ed?

Have your mum or dad ever mentioned having money to you?'

I give a bitter laugh. 'Oh yeah, I know all about the offshore millions Mum's got put away, but we're having such a good time living on the breadline that we don't want to use it.'

There's a long second of silence before Augustine clears her throat.

'Listen, me and Charlie have been thinking about what you said. If you want to go see your dad so much, then go. I'll speak to your mum and square it with her.'

I stare at her.

'That's what you want, isn't it – to see your dad?'

'Y-yes, but – I thought . . .'

'You can talk to him about how bad things are here. The fact that you and your mum are suffering because of the lack of money.'

'Dad can't do much from prison, though,' I say, starting to feel suspicious.

'You don't know what your dad might be able to do. Just make sure you tell him how bad things are. OK?'

The feeling that's been building inside me explodes as I turn on Charlie.

'STOP TELLING ME WHAT TO THINK AND WHAT TO DO!'

'Oi!' He springs up out of his seat, but Augustine pulls him back again.

She puts on her reasonable voice. 'We're not trying to tell you what to, Ed. We're—'

'You are! You, Mum, the police . . . everybody knows best for me, apparently. And him.' I turn on Charlie. 'I'm sick to death of you acting like you're my dad. You don't care about him! You're only interested in money and what you can tell the papers!'

'You little –' Charlie swipes for me, but I step back.

'There's no need for that, Ed,' Augustine says. 'Charlie's as worried as the rest of us.'

'No he isn't.' I can feel my eyes blazing, but I don't care. This stuff should've been said ages ago. 'He acts all concerned to your face, but when you're not here he's horrible to me and Sam – he's always been like that. *And* he tells lies to the press to put himself in a good light.'

'Ha, and you should know all about lying – that's a fact!'

Silence.

'It's true I've sometimes lied,' I say, my voice quieter now. 'And I shouldn't have done it, BUT . . .' I pause as they both watch me with surprised expressions. 'I've realized these past few days that there are worse liars around me, and you're one of them, Charlie Court. He's been hiding my dad's visiting orders all this time!'

'Now that's enough!' Augustine says sharply.

'You take that back, you insolent little upstart!' Charlie

is outraged, but I smile sarcastically at him, hoping that will annoy him even more.

I look away from him and stand up a bit straighter. Very calmly I say, 'Thanks, Augustine, for waiting here to tell me about Mum. I can look after her from here.'

And with that, I walk out of the house against a backdrop of Charlie's shouting insults at me, and smile. I feel so much better now.

38

Later, I'm telling Fallon and Neil about the argument with Charlie and their sudden offer to support me seeing Dad.

Fallon screws up her face. 'Why would he change his mind like that?'

'Dunno,' I say. 'But I'm not going to argue about it. Augustine is going to call our family liaison officer, Jill, to see if she can make the arrangements, but I don't know who'll take me there yet.'

Neil beckons me to sit down on the settee.

'OK, so here's an offer. If you like, I'll accompany you to the prison visiting centre to see your dad. How's that?'

'Wow . . . that would be awesome. Thanks so much, Neil.' It feels like a weight is evaporating from my shoulders as I speak.

'No problem. A boy should be able to see his dad in my opinion,' says Neil.

I nod. 'I'm worried because Charlie is really unpredictable. I don't want him changing his mind and convincing Augustine and Mum it's a bad idea.'

Neil nods. 'If you let me have Jill's number, I'll call her and offer to take you.'

It feels like a dream. Still a nightmare that Sam is

missing, but a dream that I'm closer to seeing my dad than ever before.

After a pause, I say quietly, 'It's weird because it seems people have already moved on with their lives. Even the neighbours seem to have lost interest in where Sam is. What if people think I'm more worried about Dad now?'

'I'm sure everyone is still thinking about Sam,' Fallon says kindly.

'Yes, that's true, but I mean that life just goes on as normal outside: all the shops opening, people watching stupid television programmes and talking about it on the street . . . things that used to seem so ordinary now feel so strange because, without Sam, nothing really matters any more.'

It's stuff that won't be important to anybody in twenty years' time – they'll all be worrying about something else by then.

In twenty years' time, Sam will be twenty-eight years old. If we find him.

A single tear escapes and plops down, exploding on my hand and splattering across the skin into a million tiny shards that can never be put back together into something whole again.

'Are you OK?' Fallon asks softly, and I turn my head away to hide the emotion.

'I'm fine,' I say.

'You're not fine and neither would anyone else be with

all this horror happening to you. It's OK to say it, you know.'

'Say what?' I sniff.

'To say, "I'm not all right. I'm feeling bad."'

Yeah, right.

DAY FOUR

39

The next morning, Mum comes home from hospital.

'They thought I should stay in longer, but I want to be home with you,' she says.

I feel really relieved Mum is back, but Augustine said she'd be in hospital for a few days. Mum's pale, thin face and shaking hands tell me she's probably insisted leaving far earlier than the doctors wanted her to.

'You've got to get better soon,' I say, far brighter than I feel. 'It's your birthday next week.'

Mum opens her eyes and looks at me.

'Augustine's told me about you going to visit your dad. It was Charlie who convinced me it was a bad idea for you to see him in the first place, but he seems to have changed his mind now.' Mum's voice is weary. 'If that's what you really want, Ed, then Augustine will sort it out with Jill.'

'Thanks, Mum. It is what I really want.' I press my cheek to her hot face and, for once, my heart is fluttering with joy and not nerves.

Fallon's voice calls from the back door. 'Hello?'

'Come in.' I kiss Mum's forehead and walk into the kitchen.

'Hi,' I say. 'Want a cup of tea? We've actually got some milk in this time.'

She ignores my offer. 'Can you come outside? I've got something to tell you.'

I step into the yard and she pulls the door closed behind us.

'Something weird is happening.'

I frown, not understanding.

'From my bedroom I can see right down the road,' she whispers. 'Yesterday morning I saw Charlie leave the house and walk down the street.'

'So?'

'When he got to the end of the street, he got into the passenger seat of a car that was waiting down there for him.'

'OK,' I say, not yet seeing what she's getting at.

'Then, last night, it happened again. I happened to be in my bedroom and he did the same thing. Walked down the road and got into the same red car.'

Fallon looks pleased with herself, like she's discovered something important.

'It might just be one of his drinking pals,' I say.

'But you said he's only just started going out recently. This needs investigating, Ed. Does he have a mobile phone?'

'Yes.' I nod. 'But he never leaves it lying around.'

'You're going to have to come up with a plan to make

him do just that. I need that phone for a few minutes and I can install a tracker app. That way, we can see exactly where it is he's going.'

40

Neil drives around the prison car park for what seems like ages, looking for a free space.

'There's no way we could've got a slot as fast if Jill hadn't pulled some strings,' Neil tells me.

I'd given him Jill's name yesterday before I left and he'd been able to contact her on her mobile. She'd apparently been really supportive because Neil had told her how I was struggling.

We get out of the car and my eyes are drawn to the prison block. It's a long, flat concrete building with a dark roof that presides over the car park like a mountain of doom. A wall runs round the perimeter and it's covered in wire, just like you see on TV.

It looks so cold and unfriendly, exactly the kind of place you'd prefer to stay away from. But my dad is in there and that's reason enough to push any doubts from my mind.

Neil points up at the heavy grey clouds hanging over us. 'Best get ourselves inside before the downpour, eh?' he says, and I realize I've been subconsciously dragging my feet on the approach to the prison.

I'm scared and dizzy with excitement.

Electronic doors whoosh open and as we approach the reception area my heartbeat moves up into my throat. *Thump, thump, thump.*

Neil indicates for me to sit in the waiting area as he approaches the desk. I'm terrified it will go wrong at the last minute and I won't be allowed in after all.

Neil and the receptionist have a conversation in low voices and paperwork is slid across the counter. She studies this and looks up briefly at me. I look away.

Then she smiles and speaks loud enough for me to hear her.

'Straight down the corridor and turn right at the bottom. There'll be a few security checks and then you'll be able to begin your visit in the family centre.'

'Good news,' Neil says when we begin walking towards the visiting area. 'Because you're a minor, we get to see your dad in the family centre. Much nicer than that skanky main visiting room.'

We pass through the security scanner, and then Neil pushes open the doors and we enter the family centre. It's noisy . . . and so busy. I don't know what I expected, but it's not this.

The area is large and carpeted. The walls are covered in drawings and paintings done by, I expect, the children of prisoners.

There are men, women, children, clustered together

in small groups, laughing, crying, making lots of noise. Booths are dotted around the edges of the room where some families sit quietly, talking.

I take a breath and scan the room.

And then I see him.

I see Dad.

He stands up and raises his hand. I feel my legs begin to move and I'm walking towards him. All movement around me feels like it has slowed down to a near stop. Neil is talking to me, but I can't make sense of his words.

And then suddenly, there I am. Looking up into Dad's face, and his arms fly out and wrap around me, pulling me into his chest.

'Ed,' he whispers, and even with that short, single word, his voice cracks and his mouth clamps shut.

When Dad releases me, I look at him properly for the first time in eighteen months. His clothes hang baggy on him and his hair has got much more grey in it.

'Any news?' he asks, shaking Neil's hand. 'About Sam?'

Neil shakes his head and shuffles awkwardly, looking at the floor. 'I'm going to take a walk,' he says. 'Leave you two to catch up.'

'Thanks, mate,' Dad says, and leads me over to one of the quieter booths.

I catch Neil's eye before he goes and give him a

smile. He's making himself scarce so I can talk to Dad privately.

Now the time has finally arrived, I can't stop my hands from shaking.

'It's been a long time, son,' Dad says when we sit down.

We're on opposite sides of the booth and Dad grasps my hand across the table. 'You've grown so much. You're a strapping lad now. We've got a lot of catching up to do.'

'They told me you didn't want to see me,' I tell Dad. 'But I found the visiting orders.'

There's so much I want to talk to Dad about, so much I want to ask him, but my mouth feels numb, like I've just been to the dentist.

Dad looks at his hands. 'There's so much I don't know in here, Ed. The police came to speak to me yesterday, but . . . The most important thing is, can you tell me what happened with Sam?'

I've always thought of Dad as a big, strong bloke with a deep, reassuring voice, but today he looks smaller, and his voice sounds weaker.

As I tell him what happened that day, I feel the heat of shame in my face.

'I should've taken better care of him. I should've—'

Dad shakes his head. 'You did the best you could, Ed. We all have things in our past we wish we'd done differently. I of all people know that.'

'What do you mean?'

'There are things I can't tell you because it would be dangerous for you to know, son,' he says quietly. 'I was framed by someone I trusted and that's why I'm stuck in here. But that story is for another day.'

'Your business partner?'

He nods.

'But . . . why? Why would someone do that?'

'Like I say, I can't discuss that with you right now. One day I'll tell you everything.' Dad's eyes dart around us, as if he's making sure nobody is close enough to overhear. 'I'll just say one thing – strictly between us, yeah?'

I nod.

'I'm not as stupid as some people think. I have something put by.'

'Put by?' I frown.

'Yes. I have something put by, and when I get out we'll be wealthy people.' He laces his hands on the tabletop in front of him. 'And all these years behind bars will be worth it. I've got a lot of enemies out there.'

I don't answer because to say I'm confused is an understatement. And Charlie's words about having no money float back to me: *You don't know what your dad might be able to do. Just make sure you tell him how bad things are.*

But there are far more important things at stake.

I tell Dad about Sam's note.

'I don't know what to do . . . who to tell. Mum didn't believe me. I was going to tell Augustine, but—'

'No! Don't tell her. If your mum doesn't believe you, neither will she.'

'The police, then? Sam might be in danger.'

He scowls, but says nothing.

'What is it, Dad?'

'Just . . . I don't know. Something's just occurred to me that I don't even want to think about.'

His face turns paler by the second and I wait.

'What if . . . ?'

'Yes?'

'What if someone has taken Sam to get back at *me*?'

'Why would they do that?'

Dad cups his hands over his face and his shoulders tremble.

'Where's our Sam . . . ? Where is he?' His words are muffled, but he keeps saying it, again and again, and he won't take his hands away.

I feel a clot of panic in my chest. When I came here, I felt sure Dad would have some ideas about what we could do to find Sam, but he looks as scared and hopeless as the rest of us.

Then finally, after what seems like ages, his hands drop down and he looks at me with sore, red eyes.

'I was stupid,' he says. 'I got involved back then with people who were dishonest because I was silly enough to trust them. I let myself be put in an awkward situation and then I got my fingers burned.'

He reaches for my hand again. 'My solicitor reckons that, with good behaviour, I might be out in a year, Ed. Then, I promise, I'll tell you everything. In the meantime, we've got to try to find Sam. You know him best.'

Once we get outside, I don't stop running until I reach the car. I lean against a wall, panting.

Neil runs after me, wheezing. 'Do you wish you hadn't come now?'

I shake my head. I'm glad I came – it just wasn't the outcome I'd hoped for or expected. I wanted Dad to explain why he got sent to prison, to tell me how to find Sam, but he's raised more questions than he's answered.

All sorts of things are swirling around in my head now. *I got my fingers burned . . . I've got someone watching my back.*

What did those things mean?

I feel hot and sick. Possibilities I've not even considered before now rush into my mind.

I really thought Dad wasn't to blame.

What if Dad *had* broken the law? What if he deserved to be behind bars? Worse than that, what if Dad's actions have something to do with Sam's abduction?

That had definitely occurred to Dad. I'd seen it in his face. But I got the feeling that when the truth is so upsetting, so horrible, Dad wants to just leave it be and try not to uncover it.

There's no way I'm going to do that, not any more, especially not now my brother is in danger. I'll take the truth even if it's hard to swallow. I'll take anything.

I just have to know.

41

Why can't I get what Sam said out of my head . . . *Can this den always be our secret place?* When he said that, did he know he'd be leaving me a message in his secret tin? *Did Sam know he'd be going away somewhere . . .* or am I just imagining it?

In the bathroom, I splash water on to my face and stare into the small mirror above the basin. My face looks pale and drawn; my jeans hang loose round my waist.

I try to think when I last ate a proper meal. Neil's fakeon sarnie was nice, but not really very substantial. It has been a while. I gingerly touch the dark shadows around my eyes and run a damp finger over my parched lips.

I just feel militant, like I want to cause trouble, cause a fuss, instead of agreeing to everything the people around me are fond of dictating. If I lock the bathroom door right now, I could just refuse to come out. Or I could lie down in the road until they come to take me away, throw me in hospital or take me to court.

Right now, I don't want to face people who blame us for Sam going missing.

I don't want to see Mum's pale face, lined with pain,

knowing she is only going to get worse if they don't find my brother and there is nothing at all I can do about it.

It would be wonderful to wipe my mind clean of anything and everything.

In the mirror, I take a deep breath, shake my head and turn out the light.

Lying on my bed again, I feel myself begin to drift off, the heavy mist of sleep covering me like a layer of dense fog.

Sam's face floats into my mind.

I remember his outsidey smell, his mischievous smile.

And then the vision of Sam darkens and a dark, shadowy figure looms in his place. I'm high up . . . I can't get down . . . and then Sam is back. He smiles and gives a little wave and . . . his face starts to fade.

'Don't go!' I cry. 'Stay with me.'

He's with the shadowy figure now . . . fading out further and further until I can't see him any more and everything goes black.

My own sob wakes me up.

I've just fallen asleep. Sam isn't here. Nobody is here but me.

But I think I'm starting to remember.

DAY FIVE

42

'I think you need to tell the police,' Fallon says when I tell her the next day.

'But they just think I'm a liar – that's why I haven't told them about Sam's note. Anyway, you said so yourself – we're doing a better job than the police.'

'Compromise. Tell them about the bit of memory and see how they react.'

'Will you stay while I speak to Mum?' I ask her.

She nods and we walk into the living room. Mum sits listless as ever staring into space, Augustine is reading a magazine, and Charlie is watching football.

'Mum, can I speak to you?' I say softly.

'What?' Her voice is flat and she doesn't even look at me.

'I mean, can I speak to you on your own?'

Augustine looks up from her magazine and stares pointedly at Charlie. He grabs the remote and turns the football down.

'Your mum's best staying put here, love.' Augustine smiles. 'She's sleepy after taking her tablets.'

I hesitate.

Mum looks at me. 'What is it, Ed?'

I take a deep breath and glance at Fallon. She gives me a tiny encouraging nod.

I really wanted to talk to Mum alone, but here goes . . .

'I think I remembered something,' I say. 'About Sam.'

Charlie jumps up. 'What? What did you remember?'

'Let him think, Charlie,' Augustine scolds, but she puts down her magazine.

Mum looks at me, and I notice her eyes still seem far away.

'I think someone was there when I looked over at Sam near the bushes . . . and I think Sam knew the person,' I say.

'Rubbish,' Charlie scoffs. 'He wouldn't get taken by someone he knows.'

'I want to tell the police,' I say. 'Before I forget again.'

'Tell me everything you remember.' DI Fenton sighs. His suit is shiny in places and a bit tight round his shoulders. 'And make sure it's the truth, please. We're well aware of your stories.'

I can feel heat in my cheeks, but Fallon nudges me and nods.

I tell DS Burnham what I told Mum and Charlie.

'And what makes you think that young Sam might've known this person?'

'I think he waved at him,' I say. 'He gave the person a

little wave, like when you're familiar with someone.'

'I see.' DS Burnham consults his notepad. 'It says here you were certain there was nobody about last time you were asked.'

'I couldn't remember then,' I say simply. 'It looked as though Sam was talking to the bushes and that someone must've been in there, but Sam used to talk to imaginary friends sometimes.'

'That's good news, isn't it?' Mum says to the detective. 'If Sam has gone with someone he knows.'

'Well, not necessarily,' DS Burnham says gently. 'But it's a good start.' He turns to me again. 'Ed, can you be certain you saw someone with Sam over by the bushes?'

I can't. I can't be absolutely certain.

An urge to make something up fills my chest. I'm under pressure and it's so much easier to just tell them what they want to hear, that I am certain of what I'm saying.

But this time I pause before I speak and look at Fallon. She watches me.

'No, I can't be certain,' I say. 'But I think it might be a memory coming back. Soon, I might be certain.'

'You seem really unsure, Sam.' Augustine smiles at the detectives. 'I think he's a bit confused.'

'For God's sake,' Charlie snaps. 'Don't tell me we've dragged the detectives here for nothing.'

DI Fenton shuffles to the edge of his seat and peers

231

at me in a stern manner.

'Do you want your brother back home, Ed?'

'Course I do!' What a stupid question.

'Then you need to think very carefully about what "memories" surface. There's a big difference between made-up stories and genuine memories, and you could end up doing this investigation more harm than good if it sends us off on a wild-goose chase.'

I bite my lip to stop myself shouting at him. I almost wish I'd never said anything. But it's the truth . . . I do believe something is coming back.

'Ed thought it was the right thing to do,' Fallon says quietly. 'To tell the police.'

'And it is. Just so long as it's not one of Ed's elaborate stories.' DS Burnham stands up. 'If you remember anything else, I suggest you have a good think before letting us know.'

I stand up and stride across the room. I hear Fallon behind me. We walk out of the house and into the garden.

And, like an idiot, I burst into tears. 'I just need air,' I say, gulping back an embarrassing sob. 'They didn't believe me.'

'It's my fault for encouraging you to tell the police.' Fallon scowls. 'I didn't realize they'd already made their minds up that you tell lies constantly.'

'For once I tell the truth and this is what happens,' I say.

'You can't exactly blame people,' Fallon points out. 'You know *The Boy Who Cried Wolf* story, right?'

'Yeah, I know.' I shrug. 'I'm gonna just take a little walk, try to get my thoughts in order.'

When Fallon goes home, I walk to the park and just sit there for hours, skimming stones across the pond. I visit the den on the way down, but it's the same as I left it. No more notes.

My entire body aches with tiredness and it's getting dark outside, but, even so, I don't want to go back inside and face Mum and Charlie. It's clear they both think I'm lying to the police.

I've just turned the corner of our street when I hear a crunching noise behind me, like boots on gravel.

Before I can turn round, I feel a low blow to my back followed by a really hard push. I lose my balance, careering into the shadows. My shoulder hits a brick wall full-on.

I groan and sink down to my haunches, rubbing at my arm.

A heavy boot slams into my leg and I cry out.

Then . . . a man's voice issues a gruff threat: 'Keep your nose out of stuff that doesn't concern you.'

I don't recognize the voice. I squint, willing my eyes to adjust to the gloom.

I look up, but his face is shrouded behind a hooded top.

The growl of an engine makes me jump. I turn my head just in time to see a red car disappearing around the corner. It looks familiar . . . But my leg is hurting and I can't make sense of the misty images in my head.

The figure takes a step back as though he is readying himself to administer another kick, and I cry out, 'Who – who are you?' and scramble to my feet.

He watches me. 'You've been warned,' he growls. 'Things aren't what you think they are. Stop meddling.' Then he disappears.

I limp out of the gloom, looking all around for a sign he's still around, but nobody is there now.

'Things aren't what you think they are.'

What's that supposed to mean? And was he talking about my visit to Dad or speaking to the police about Sam?

There's a lot I don't know, but something here just doesn't fit.

I limp straight back home. Charlie is texting on his phone. He looks up and gives me a strange smile.

'What happened to you?' he says, smirking. 'You'll be telling the police you got attacked next.'

I consider telling him what happened, but decide there's no point.

A terrible thought begins to form in my head.

Could Charlie have somehow been to blame for Dad being arrested?

I close my bedroom door behind me quietly and look out into the darkness.

I can't bear the night-times. If Mum stopped breathing with grief, how would I know?

Dread coats my tongue like a layer of thick, green mould.

I hear a door slam downstairs, and when I look down into the yard I see Charlie is going out again. I think about Fallon's suspicions that he's up to no good.

I pace around my bedroom, thinking.

I go back downstairs and look out of the living-room window at the small, tired patch of grass that has been scattered with somebody else's litter. Over the bony hedge and the other side of the street, a tattered England flag flaps half-heartedly from a first-floor window in the light breeze, its colours long bleached out.

A picture of a red car driving slowly by the house pops into my head. What does it mean? I try and mentally grasp the image and then, at last, it clicks . . . Fallon said she'd seen Charlie get in a red car!

But there's something more niggling at me. The car seems significant. That snippet of memory I have of a red car driving slowly by our house. Could it be connected to the mysterious things I'd told Imran just before Sam went missing – someone watching the house?

There are just three people hanging around outside now – diehard press who still think there's a chance of something worthwhile happening that could sell a few newspapers.

The old elm tree over the road stands proud, no matter what the weather is doing. The pavement around its roots has buckled, slowly yielding to its might.

The leaves on the tree shimmer like little butterfly wings in the glow from the streetlights. If I were a leaf, I'd want to sit at the top of the tree, but you can't always choose where you end up.

Something flashes in front of my eyes, like a firework. It's an image . . . of Sam walking away with someone. He's looking up at the person and talking. He is holding their hand.

He turns round and smiles at me. Waves.

Sam was happy to leave the park with whoever held his hand.

43

I go straight next door to tell Fallon about the new
memories and also about being attacked. Her face pales.

'If it's the same red car, then Charlie has been out
every day and got in it, Ed. He might know the person
who's attacked you. We need to find out where it is he is
going for hours on end. I just need five minutes with his
phone. I'll explain why, later.'

When Charlie is making a sandwich in the kitchen, I slip
outside and call Fallon. She waits outside the kitchen door
and I go back inside and make myself a drink.

I wait until he puts his phone down on the worktop
and move towards him, a long glass of orange cordial in
my hand. As he's about to turn round, I barge into him.
The cordial flies everywhere, but mostly over Charlie.

'You bloody idiot!' he screams. 'I'm going out soon and
now look . . . I'm drenched!'

'Sorry, Charlie,' I say, pasting a remorseful look on my
face.

He pushes past me and slams the kitchen door behind
him hard. I hear him stomping upstairs. I snatch up
his phone and open the door. Fallon slips inside and

begins tapping on the screen.

'Good job he just put it down and went off in a huff,' she whispers. 'I don't have to go through the password lock.'

The kitchen falls silent. We look at each other, our faces flushed with nerves.

'How long?' I hiss. I can hear Charlie moving around upstairs. He's probably just slipping on a dry T-shirt.

'A few more minutes,' she says. 'It's just downloading.'

A door opens and closes upstairs. Then footsteps. Charlie is coming back downstairs. I wipe my forehead where little beads of sweat are forming.

Fallon throws me a look and I rush into the hallway and close the kitchen door behind me. Charlie gets to the bottom of the stairs and frowns.

'Did you get changed?' I say.

He tugs the bottom of his T-shirt. 'Different colour, or haven't you noticed?'

He steps forward towards the kitchen door, but I don't budge.

'I'm really sorry about the drink,' I say. 'I just wasn't paying attention.'

'Yeah, well. Be careful in future. Move, then.'

He tries to go round me to get to the door, and I skip to each side like a shadow boxer so he can't.

'Have you lost your marbles?' He glances at his watch. 'Move out of the way, you daft bugger. I want to eat my sandwich, then I've somewhere to be.'

'Are you going anywhere nice?' I ask.

'What?'

'When you go out, I mean.'

'What's it got to do with you?' His expression becomes a snarl. 'Move, or I'll knock you out of the way.'

My heart is thumping a crazy rhythm in my chest. Charlie is going to find Fallon with his phone and . . . I can't even imagine how angry he'll be. I feel sick at the thought of him losing his temper.

'It's just . . . there's something I wanted to tell you,' I say.

He looks surprised. 'What's that, then?'

I'm shifting about, one foot to the other. I'm trying desperately to think of an excuse if Charlie catches us in the act, but nothing remotely convincing will come.

'I think I've had another memory.'

'Oh, give it a rest.'

He shoves me just as the kitchen door opens behind me.

'Only me,' Fallon calls. 'Just popped round to see how your mum is, Ed.'

I breathe a sigh of relief and stand aside. Fallon nods quickly at me, meaning she had success.

Charlie pushes roughly past me, muttering. He heads straight over to the worktop and snatches up his phone.

He glances at the screen and then takes a massive bite of his sandwich.

'So, what's this memory you had, then?' he says with his mouth full.

'It doesn't matter now,' I say.

He shakes his head. 'Make your bloody mind up.'

Five minutes later, he leaves the house without saying goodbye.

44

Fallon gets out her own phone and presses a button.

'See that moving red dot?' She shows me a map and I nod. 'That's Charlie. The green dot here that's not moving – that's us. All we have to do is watch and he'll lead us straight to where he's going.'

We lean over the screen and watch as the red dot, Charlie, moves away from the house.

'He's just walking down the road,' Fallon says. 'Now watch.'

The red dot appears to stop for a few moments and then, all of a sudden, it takes off and moves faster and faster, away from us.

'He's in the car now,' Fallon says, a little breathless. 'Now we just have to see where he takes us.'

She expands the map so it shows a bigger area. The red dot is moving rapidly now, along what I can see is the main road leading out of town.

'It looks like he's heading towards the open countryside out towards Newark,' I say.

'Why would he be going there?'

'I've no idea.' I bite my lip. 'He doesn't fish or walk. I wonder whose car he's in.'

'I don't know. I can't answer that question, but I can tell you it's a red Ford Escort.' Fallon grins. 'And I wrote down the number plate just in case we need to give it to the police.'

We watch as the red dot inches its way across the screen.

'I think they're slowing down,' Fallon says. 'They're in the middle of nowhere.' The dot stops moving. 'Now we just have to wait and see how long they stay there.'

An hour later, the dot still hasn't moved.

'We're going to have to go out there,' Fallon says.

'But how? We've nobody to drive us and it's not exactly a popular bus route, the middle of a clump of fields.'

'I've got a bike, and you can borrow my dad's,' Fallon says. 'Tomorrow, we're going to follow him. I've saved a green pin on the map there so we know the exact location. We don't have to keep up with the red car, but we can't leave before it or they might see us.'

Forty minutes later, we're getting fidgety just watching with nothing happening.

'What can they be doing out there?' I grumble.

'Look!'

Fallon points at the screen as the red dot starts to move again.

'He's on his way back,' she says.

DAY SIX

45

The next morning, I lie awake waiting for daylight. I feel as if I've literally been awake the whole night wondering if this is the day Sam will be found.

Soon as I can slip out of the house, I go round to Fallon's, and an hour after waking, I find myself a few streets away from ours, riding Fallon's dad's bike up and down.

'You'd better sort yourself out.' She laughs. 'We've got miles to cycle.'

'It's ages since I've ridden a bike,' I say, trying to defend myself.

'It's the kind of thing you never forget,' Fallon says. 'Have a bit of a practice and then we'll get off.'

After about another five or ten minutes, although I'm still a bit wobbly, at least I'm moving at a reasonable pace.

'We know exactly where Charlie is going, and he's left about the same time each day,' Fallon says. 'If we get off now, we should be able to get there before them.'

We cycle for about forty minutes or so.

'Let's stop for a rest,' I pant.

'What's wrong with you? We've got ages to go yet.'

'I know, but it's made me realize how unfit I am,' I say breathlessly.

'Come on, Ed. I've just got this feeling that something important is going to change today.'

'In what way?'

'I don't know,' she calls back to me as we set off again. 'It's just a feeling.'

After another twenty minutes, we stop for Fallon to look at her phone.

'He's still at your house at the moment,' she says. 'He should be setting off pretty soon, though. Come on, we'll take it steady, but we need to get out there.

Soon, the landscape changes. Shops and houses seem to fade and open countryside replaces the urban scenes.

'We're not too far now,' Fallon calls back. 'Maybe three miles at the most.'

Fortunately, there aren't too many hills. Still, my thigh muscles burn and I seem to be constantly out of breath. We haven't brought any water, but I just try to focus on what we might find out . . .

'We're pretty close now,' Fallon says. 'And look.' She stops cycling and shows me the map. The red dot is on the move and about halfway between the green dot, us and home. 'It's only about half a mile now; we're really close to the location they were at yesterday.'

'But there's absolutely nothing here,' I exclaim, taking in all the greenery and hedgerows around us. 'Why on earth would Charlie want to come out here for two hours every day?'

Another ten minutes and Fallon stops cycling, gets off her bike.

'Quickly,' she says. 'Wheel the bikes behind this hedge.'

When we're out of sight of the narrow road, Fallon looks at her phone screen and whispers, 'They'll be passing us any time now. Crouch well down.'

The red Ford Escort passes us. It isn't going too fast and when I peer through the branches and leaves of the hedge, I see Charlie with another man who is driving the car. They seem deep in conversation, looking straight ahead instead of in our direction.

'Do you recognize the driver?' Fallon says.

'Never seen him before,' I say. 'Let's wait until the car is out of sight at the end of this lane and then we can follow.'

Soon, there's no sign of the vehicle.

'Wherever they're heading to is literally just round that bend at the top,' Fallon says. 'If they're going to the same place as yesterday, which I think they are.'

We quickly get the bikes back on the road and start cycling.

'We've got to be really careful now,' Fallon calls as we approach the bend. 'It's just around here.'

We get off the bikes and push them to the bend.

'Wait here,' I say, and Fallon takes the handlebars of my bike. 'I'll creep around the bend behind the hedge and see what's out there.'

I climb into the field and stick close to the hedge as it follows the bend in the road, crouching down and shuffling along like a crab.

Suddenly, a stone-built farmhouse looms up. I remember seeing it on the map but had somehow missed that it's the only building around here. It's old and looks in need of some repair. The red car is parked outside and there's nobody in it. They must already be inside.

'Fallon,' I hiss. 'Come on! Lie the bikes down here and we'll go on foot.'

A few seconds later, she appears at my side.

'Come on, then,' she breathes. 'Time for us to find out what Charlie is up to.'

46

We stick to the hedgerow as far as we can before the leafy cover ends and we're forced to run across the road and into the farmhouse yard.

Dashing across as quickly as possible, we crouch behind the red car parked there.

'Let's wait here a few seconds,' I whisper. 'Watch out for any movement or if we can hear anything.'

Fallon nods. There's nothing to see and no sounds apart from birdsong and the faint rumble of the odd distant lorry.

'Follow me.' I run from the side of the car to the farmhouse wall. Fallon is just a step behind until we stand by the door. If anyone comes out of the building, we have nowhere to hide.

My heart feels like it's going to explode if it beats much faster. My mouth is dry and I feel as if I could cough at any second, but I just try to calm my breathing.

Fallon doesn't speak. I can see her eyes are wide, her shoulders tense, and I know she's as scared as I am.

We see nothing, hear nothing. If it wasn't for the car outside, the place would look completely empty. But we know better.

Very, very slowly, I reach for the handle of the peeling brown door and with a shaking hand push it downwards. They've left it unlocked, thinking there was nobody around here for miles, I suppose.

The door opens without a squeak, and Fallon follows me inside. We're in what would have been the kitchen of the farmhouse. It doesn't look as though anybody has lived here for a long, long time. The terracotta tiled floor is dull and echoey beneath our feet, and I feel so relieved we're both wearing trainers.

I leave the door open behind us a moment while I listen again for any sounds, but it's clear that the downstairs is empty. Then we hear footsteps above us.

Charlie must be on the first floor.

We creep to the side of a long cupboard. The hinges are ruined and the door is hanging off it, but it's big enough to offer a hiding place if they decide to come downstairs suddenly.

We hear voices and more footsteps. I signal to Fallon to leave the side of the cupboard and move towards the stairs that I can see snaking upwards.

'We've got no choice,' I whisper. 'We can't stay down here; we need to see what they're up to!'

'We can't!' Fallon's eyes widen further. 'They'll see us . . . They're bound to!'

'I'll go first, but if it looks like I'm going to get caught, you just run out of here and call 999 as soon as possible.'

'OK.' She nods, biting her bottom lip.

It's the first time I've seen her look as petrified as me, but we've come this far – we *have* to find out what is happening now.

I begin to creep upstairs. I stick to the edges where there is less chance of creaks, the talking upstairs masking any of the faint sounds I make.

I can see doors leading off from the landing. Most are slightly ajar, but then the voices grow louder and I know they are in the end room.

And that's when I hear it.

A child's voice.

47

Sam's voice . . . My brother is up there!

I gasp and look at Fallon, and mouth the word, 'Sam!'

Her hand flies to her mouth and she shakes her head in denial. I mime tapping the phone for her to call the police as we agreed and she nods and tiptoes back downstairs.

I creep along the landing, trying to steal a look into the room where the voices are coming from. The door is slightly open, but I haven't got a clear view in there.

Once I get outside it, I peer through the crack where the hinges are and my eyes fill with tears. I can see Sam! He seems OK, lots of toys around him. He's a bit pale and looks thinner . . . but he's really OK.

Charlie is crouched in front of him, talking to him and being really nice. He tells him he'll take him to the play park when he gets back home and that he's going to buy him a proper John Deere tractor especially for young farmers.

But Sam starts to cry.

'I hate you! I don't want to go to the park—'

His words cut off suddenly as Charlie roughly places his hand over Sam's mouth.

I step forward, ready to run at Charlie, get him away

from my brother any way I can, but suddenly my feet freeze when there is movement over the other side of the room and I realize there's not just Charlie and the driver in the room . . . but three people.

There's a woman! She stands with her back to me and then starts to turn, very slowly, and I swear my heart nearly stops as the realization of who she is hits me.

I gasp out loud and all three of them turn round.

'Get him!' Charlie yells.

48

In a panicky instinct, I turn to run and then stop dead. I'm not going anywhere.

I won't leave Sam alone. It's my chance to make amends for when he went first missing at the park.

The driver of the red car dashes out and grabs me roughly in a bear hug.

'Get off me!' I yell, trying desperately to wriggle out of his iron grip.

'Get in there,' he growls, pushing me into the room.

That voice – it's the one that threatened me, attacked me last night. It's the voice that warned me about meddling in things that didn't concern me. Charlie's friend.

'Ed! Ed!' Sam's little voice calls out. 'Help me!'

'What's wrong with you? You've been treated like a little prince in here, you spoilt little brat,' Charlie snaps at Sam.

'Don't speak to him like that!' I shout at him.

'Right live wire this one, ain't he?' The driver laughs, batting me round the head with the flat of his hand.

I pull away from his one-handed grasp and rush over to my brother, flinging my arms round him and pulling him close.

He sobs into my chest and tears roll down my own cheeks.

'Oh, please . . . spare us the dramatics.' Charlie pulls a face.

For a second or two, I'm lost in the relief, the joy of finding Sam unharmed, and then a trickle of dread traces up my spine as I feel the eyes of someone on my back and I know it's time to face the awful truth.

I turn slowly and I glare at the one person in the room who has said nothing. The one who is standing back in the shadows, watching with a chilling detachment.

The most dangerous person in here.

'Augustine. I can't believe it's been you all along,' I say slowly. 'Charlie, yes. But not you. You're Mum's best friend; you've looked after Sam since he was a baby, been there when Mum was ill. *How could you?*'

I see the briefest flicker of an emotion on her face . . . shame or regret? I can't tell, but in a heartbeat it is gone. Something else . . . arrogance . . . seems to take over, and she throws her shoulders back.

'Had to be done.' She smirks. 'You're just a kid. You could never understand.'

Sam's arms tighten round me as I stand up, stumbling back from them with Sam still clutched to my side. I scramble towards the wall, hold on to it as dizziness and nausea flood my body.

Something seems to explode in my brain. Flashes of

moving images flick like a slideshow in front of me.

The room, the people . . . they fade away and suddenly I'm back there at the park . . .

I was sitting on the top of the climbing frame, balancing on the two thinnest bits, when I saw Sam talking near the swings.

At first, I thought he was just talking to himself, but then I saw he was kind of talking into the bushes, like there was someone hiding in there.

'Sam,' I called down to him. 'Come here. NOW.' But he ignored me, just carried on talking to the bushes.

I shouted again and this time he glanced up at me and I saw the bushes rustle and move like there was someone in there, watching us.

I yelled, loud as I could, 'Hey! What are you up to over there?'

But my brother didn't even turn round. 'Hide and seek!' he yelled in delight.

Augustine leaned forward and said something to Sam. She looked over at me and I waved as she held out her hand to Sam.

Sam smiled, waved to me as he walked away, clutching Augustine's hand.

I started to get down from the frame when I spotted a man climbing out of the bushes to follow them . . . he wore a hooded top and I noticed he was unshaven. He looked around shiftily before setting off behind Sam and Augustine.

I wobbled in my panic and lost my balance on the play equipment.

'It was you, all along . . .' I whisper to Augustine.

'Don't blame me – blame that father of yours.'

'What's Dad got to do with this?'

'He's the one that ruined my business, just because he didn't like the thought of using foreign nationals as cheap labour.'

'What?' The awful truth suddenly dawns on me. '*You're* Dad's business partner?'

'I *was* your dad's business partner,' she spat. 'Until he ruined everything.'

All this time I've been wondering who Dad's mystery partner was, and she's been here, right under my nose.

'Augustine had a nice little set-up going until your loser father ruined everything,' Charlie adds.

I look from one to the other, trying to keep up with the revelations.

Augustine nods. 'Charlie was in the business with me.'

'You two knew each other? You didn't meet down at the pub the night you were with Mum?'

Charlie grins and claps his hands slowly. 'Give the boy a prize.'

'Shut it, stupid,' Augustine snarls at him.

'*Why?* Why would you do this to Mum?' I say faintly. I feel so tired all of a sudden, like everything that seemed real is dissolving before my eyes. 'Mum loves you. *We* love you . . .'

'Because there's a hundred thousand pounds that's been taken from my business and hidden somewhere. It belongs to me, and your dad knows where it is, I'm certain of it.'

Dad must have hidden the money!

'We've tried everything to find out where that cash is, but of course nobody is owning up to it,' Augustine says.

'We were left no choice but to take Sam to try and force your dad to tell us.' Charlie clenches his jaw. 'Now the press attention has died down, we're going to send out a ransom notice for a hundred grand tomorrow, and you're not going to ruin that, you little prat.'

'Don't worry, Sam.' I squeeze him closer. 'I'm not going anywhere.'

'Too right you're not.' Charlie laughs. He turns to the driver. 'Take him down to the cellar. Leave the other kid here.'

'No!' Sam screams.

I try to fight the driver off with one arm, but he grabs me easily and drags me away from my brother.

'Wait! What's that noise?' Augustine runs to the window. 'Oh my God . . . it's the police! How can they have known . . . ?'

Fallon!

DAY SEVEN

49

I'm sitting in a small rowing boat on a peaceful lake. There is nobody else around.

I look for my oars to start paddling to the bank, but they've gone, fallen into the water.

'Ed?' I feel a gentle shaking on my arm and the lake fades away.

My mind clears quickly and I remember everything in an instant. The entire mess of it.

When I open my eyes, Fallon is standing at the side of the settee, looking down on me. She sits down next to me and looks at me, but she doesn't say anything. Her eyes keep flicking away and then back to me again as if she is unsure about my reaction.

I look back at her and I start to feel a little calmer inside.

'W-where's Sam?' I stammer.

'Don't worry – he's fine.' She smiles. 'He's with your mum. They're asleep upstairs.'

I feel sort of different inside.

Emptier.

All those times I've tried to talk to her, but it wasn't the right time, wasn't the right day.

All those times I've been convinced she was keeping

263

the truth about what happened to Dad from me for no good reason.

Mum had been just as much in the dark as I was.

More than a week later, I still couldn't stay in the house for long. Not at first.

The story unfolded and there was still a surprise in store.

DS Burnham sat us down the day after we found Sam and tried to explain.

'Charlie helped Augustine run the illegal clothing factory that employed people who'd come here for a better life but hadn't yet got their papers. She forced them to work for pennies or she would expose them to the authorities.'

'Dad wanted to be part of that business?' I frowned.

'He says he didn't know it was an illegal operation, and we believe him,' the detective told us. 'Soon as he found out, he tried to back out of the deal, but Augustine and Charlie said if he didn't go along with their plan they'd frame him for employing immigrants without papers.'

'It seems your dad had built up a bit of a nest egg and then told them he wanted nothing more to do with it,' Mum said. 'So Augustine and Charlie carried out their threat and got your dad sent to prison.'

'What they didn't realize, at first, is that he'd also tucked away a nice little lump sum from the business . . . most of it money to pay their fabric suppliers,' DS Burnham continued. 'They would have made a lot of money if it had continued, but the money your dad took was already spoken for.'

'Where is it, then? Where's the money?'

'Ahh,' DS Burnham glanced at Mum. 'The question we'd all like answering.'

TWO
MONTHS
LATER

TWO
MONTHS
LATER

50

Sometimes, I want Dad to know how selfish and unfair he's been.

Getting involved in a dodgy business deal and leaving Mum with the fall-out. Not to mention taking money that didn't belong to him . . . but, when it all came out, Dad did the right thing and told the police about the money, handed it all over.

But always, without fail, a wave of sadness kills the anger, almost as quickly as it flashes up. Most of all, I can never match the dad who always loved me so much with this person who'd acted like that.

Virtually everything Dad did, he did for us. Even when I saw him struggling with his migraines when I was younger – that I now understood were migraines from the pressure of it all – he fought against it.

'How could Dad have messed things up so badly?' I say to Fallon one day when we're out walking.

'I don't know.'

Fallon has been by my side since the day we found Sam.

We've done a lot of walking, and she's done a lot of

listening, but she hasn't said much. Which, somehow, has helped.

Two plain hairgrips hold the red dreadlocks back from her face, and her ears stick out a bit. I like the fact that she doesn't mind me seeing who she really is, that she doesn't try to cover anything up. Fallon is my friend and I trust her more than anyone.

Imran's mum sent a card, and Imran put a note in it, inviting me over. I'm going to accept.

When I get back home from our walk, I put the key in the lock of the back door and feel a rush of sickness when I realize it is already open.

We've been strict about keeping the door locked since the full story came out. Our front gate is a magnet for local and national press once more.

I push open the door and I'm about to call out to Mum and Sam when I hear voices.

Mum's voice – and a man's voice.

I walk softly through the kitchen and into the hallway, holding my breath.

I listen harder, my ears twitching in shock.

I must be mistaken. It can't be *him*.

Walking through the living-room door, every part of me prickles with goosebumps.

As I get closer, I realize I am right. It *is* him. Of course, I recognize the voice, but I can't process what he is saying. I can't handle that he is actually here.

I push the living-room door fully open and stand there looking straight at him.

'Hello, Ed,' Dad says, standing up.

Mum looks at him and then she looks at me. Sam lets go of Dad's hand and runs across the room to me, clinging on to my waist.

Her face looks worn and sad. She swallows, but doesn't say anything.

'Dad?'

'Your dad came to see me of his own accord,' Mum says. 'To tell me what happened in his own words.'

Dad's hair is combed neatly back and he is clean-shaven. He comes over and puts his arm round me.

'They let me out because Augustine and Charlie admitted to framing me for the factory thing,' he says.

'Are you coming back home?' Sam asks.

Dad coughs and looks at Mum. He has on the same clothes as when I visited him, but they look like they've had a wash.

'I'll get off now. I know you all have things to talk about,' Dad says.

I don't say anything to him because I don't know what to say. I'm glad Dad is out of prison and we have a lot to talk about. I feel a mixture of so many emotions, I can't speak.

I stand aside and as he passes me, he brushes his hand briefly across my shoulder. I breathe in and smell his clean soap smell.

When I hear Dad close the door behind me, I walk into the kitchen to lock up again.

I stand for a minute or two in there, take some deep breaths and bite my bottom lip, trying to think.

My mind is a maze of painful feelings, betrayal, lies and not much truth. But, of course, I know all about that. You can tell all the stories in the world, but it doesn't take the truth away.

Then I walk slowly back to the living room.

Mum is crying. 'I've done you wrong and I've done myself wrong too in refusing to talk about your dad. We should have discussed your worries, not hidden him away like a guilty secret.'

For a moment I feel like I've floated out of my body and I'm watching us both. This moment that I've waited so long for, it is finally here.

She takes a breath.

'See, Ed, for a long time I felt really angry with your dad for what he did. I felt angry at him for leaving the three of us by getting himself sent down.'

'I've always known something was wrong about what happened,' I say slowly, looking out of the window, 'but you'd never talk about it. It was never the right time.'

'Your dad was always a good man. A man who did

what he thought was best for his family,' she says. 'I never meant to wipe the memory of him from our lives.'

I think about the times I've seen *that look* on her face when I've mentioned Dad. Now I understand it wasn't me she was angry at.

I don't say anything.

'If I'm honest, there are times I do blame him. Maybe part of me always will,' she says. 'It doesn't seem to get any easier, and now it's your problem to struggle with too.'

I've begged Mum to be honest with me for a long time and yet what she says is still hard to swallow.

'Sometimes, in this life, things don't always turn out the way we expect or want them to,' Mum says, gazing at her quivering hands. 'Despite my best intentions, there are times I've still felt bitter and frustrated about your dad leaving us alone. And it's been so hard to cope. I'm sorry you had to see that, Ed.'

I press my lips together.

'Sometimes I've felt bitter and frustrated too,' I whisper. 'I admit there have been times I've said anything . . . made up stuff . . . just to tell a better story that everyone wants to hear. But I've learned other people do it too. Newspapers do it every day and call it journalism.'

Mum nods. 'It's true. We all find different ways to run from the truth, some more obvious than others.'

I think for a moment. 'Now, I'm not so scared of the

truth. I can say what I want to say, and if people don't like it then . . . that's up to them.'

As I say the words, I realize that speaking the truth feels so much better than thinking up yet another story. Right now, it feels good to just *be myself*.

And, for once, I really mean it.

Acknowledgements

Producing a finished book takes the help and support of a lot of talented and committed people. Fortunately for me, I have some of the best in my team!

I'd like to give a special thank you to Lucy Pearse at Macmillan for her insight and encouragement during the editing process of *The Boy Who Lied* and for helping to make the book the best it can be.

Huge thanks to the whole team at Macmillan Children's Books, especially to Rachel Vale and the MCB design department and to illustrator Helen Crawford-White.

Thank you to my agent, Clare Wallace for her tireless support and to everyone at Darley Anderson Children's Agency, especially Mary Darby and Emma Winter for their work in getting my Young Adult stories out into the world.

Enormous thanks to Nigel Adams, Director of Hope Nottingham, a Christian charity working with local churches and community groups to serve those in need. Nigel kindly showed me around the Hope Cafe and food bank situated in Hope House in Beeston, Nottingham and this really helped my understanding when writing the book. It was wonderful to see the work being done there in helping people to make a lasting transformation in their lives.

You can find out more about the work of Hope Nottingham at www.hope-nottingham.org.uk.

Heartfelt thanks to the wonderful librarians and booksellers who support and recommend my books and to my young readers who are always so full of enthusiasm and amazing questions when I visit them in schools and academies! Thanks also to the organisers of the many varied and extremely important book awards that get young people reading and trying out new genres.

Huge thanks as always go to my daughter, Francesca, and Mum, Christine, who always believed I would be published from the earliest days and especially to my husband Mac, for his constant support and unswerving belief in me.

Special thanks to my Dad, Harry, who knows Bulwell very well and recently took me out on a trip to visit old haunts which helped me when writing the setting.

I lived on Muriel Street when I was very young, my Dad grew up on Grindon Crescent as a child and my Mum on Longford Crescent and my beloved nana lived on Radley Square . . . so it was a trip with happy family memories and lots of stories!

As a child, my dad used to take me to Bulwell Hall Park on a Sunday where I loved kind-fishing for sticklebacks, just like Sam. It's changed an awful lot so readers who know Bulwell, bear in mind I wrote what I saw in my memories!

All my books are set in Nottinghamshire, the place I was born and have lived all my life. Local readers should be aware I sometimes take the liberty of changing street names or geographical details to suit the story.

If you would like more information about or help with any of the issues covered in the book there are many excellent resources that can be accessed by searching online or, alternatively, ask a parent, teacher or librarian for help.

Finally, thank YOU for reading *The Boy Who Lied*! Please see my website to keep up to speed with my latest writing news.

www.kimslater.com

Read on for an exclusive extract from *Smart*

A mysterious crime,
a different detective

SMART

KIM SLATER

'A remarkable first novel' *Guardian*

①

DEAD IN THE WATER

It just looked like a pile of rags, floating on the water.

Jean sat on the bench with the brass plaque on. It said: *In Memory of Norman Reeves, who spent many happy hours here.*

The plaque means Norman Reeves is dead, but it doesn't actually say that.

Jean held her head in her hands and her body was all jerky, like when you are laughing or crying. I guessed she was crying and I was right.

'He was my friend,' she sobbed.

I looked around but Jean was alone. People around here say Jean is 'cuckoo'. That means mental. She used to be a nurse that delivered babies. She still knows loads of stuff she learned from medical books but no one believes her.

'Who?' I asked.

Jean pointed to the rags.

I went to the edge of the embankment to look. There was a stripy bag half in the water. I saw a face with a bushy beard in the middle of the rags, under the ripples. One eye was open, one was closed.

I freaked out. The sea sound started in my head and I ran right past the bridge and back again but there was nobody to help. I'm not supposed to run like mad because it can start my asthma off.

'When the sea noise comes in your head,' Miss Crane says, 'it is important to stay calm and breathe.'

I stopped running. I tried to stay calm and breathe. I used my inhaler.

Jean was still crying when I got back.

'He was my friend,' she said again. I picked up a long stick and took it over to the riverbank. I poked at the face but not near the eyes.

'What are you doing?' Jean shouted from the bench.

'I'm doing a test to see if it's a balloon,' I yelled back. It felt puffy and hard at the same time, so I knew it was Jean's friend's head.

'Is it a balloon?' shouted Jean.

A woman with a dog was coming.

When she got near I said, 'Jean's friend is in the river.'

She gave me a funny look, like she might ignore me and carry on walking. Then she came a bit nearer and looked at the river. She started screaming.

I went for a walk up the embankment to stay calm and breathe. Some Canada geese flew down and skidded into the water. They didn't care about the rags and the puffy face. They just got on with it.

When I got back, a policeman and a policewoman were talking to the lady with the dog. Jean was still sitting on the bench but nobody was talking to her.

'That's him,' the woman said, and pointed at me.

'What's your name, son?' The policeman asked.

'I'm not your son,' I said. 'My dad is dead from a disease that made him drink cider, even in the morning.'

The policeman and the policewoman looked at each other.

'Can you tell us what happened, love?' The policewoman had a kind face, like Mum when she wasn't rushing to go to work. She nodded her head towards the river. 'Is that how you found him?'

'It looked like rags,' I said.

'He was my friend,' Jean shouted from the bench.

The policewoman wrote down my name and address.

'Was he just like this, when you got here?' asked the policeman.

'The head was a bit more turned towards the bridge,' I said. 'Before I poked it with the stick.'

'Stick?'

'I had to see if it was a balloon or a real head,' I said.

The woman with the dog shrieked. She even made the policewoman jump.

'It's definitely a real head,' I said.

'Did you see anyone else around here but the tramp lady?' asked the policeman.

'Jean was a nurse,' I said. 'She's not mental.'

A white van pulled up. It had the words *Police Diving Unit* on the side and a blue flashing light. Even when it stood still, the light kept flashing.

'Kieran,' said the policeman. 'Did you see anyone else hanging around here?'

'No,' I said. 'How many divers will go in?'

The side of the van slid back and two police divers got out. They had flippers on and everything.

'They'll need breathing apparatus on if they're going to search the water for clues,' I said.

'No need for that,' the policewoman said in a low voice, like she didn't want me to hear. 'Poor old bogger probably fell in after one too many.'

A man got out of the front of the police van and took some photographs of Jean's friend in the water. Then the divers put up some screens while they pulled the body out of the river.

'Why are they hiding it?' I said. 'I've already seen it.'

'And poked it,' said the policeman as they moved away. 'Don't go touching dead bodies in future.'

There were some people gathering on the far bank. One man had binoculars.

The police emptied the dead man's stripy bag and spread the things out on the concrete. There was a blanket, some socks and an empty packet of cheese straws.

Two older boys from my school walked up and stood watching.

'What you been up to, Downs? You topped somebody?' asked one of them.

'I haven't got Down's,' I said. 'There's nothing wrong with my chromosomes.'

'Are you sure about that, Downs?' asked the other boy.

They fell about laughing.

②

THE LETTER

One day I'm going to be a reporter for the *Evening Post*. That's why I started walking straight home, so I could write stuff down.

I don't write in my notebook all the time. I used to only write in it when bad things happened, like when Grandma stopped coming round.

But now I write down all the interesting things that happen too, so the Editor of the *Post* will want me to work for him when I leave school. I can show him my notebook as evidence of my reporting skills.

The bad thing at the river was definitely interesting.

I can do the tiniest writing in the world; even I can't read it sometimes. Nobody can tell other people what I've said, which is the best thing. You can't trust people but you can trust your notebook.

I ripped out all the pages of my old *Beano* annual and I hide my notebook in there. Then I put the annual in the middle of a pile of other annuals under the bed. Nobody will ever find it.

See, this is why I like writing in my notebook. I can talk about anything that's ever been invented and no one can tell me off.

I. Am. In. Charge.

You can write sentences with only one word in them, like that. It's your choice.

I live in Nottingham. Not right in the middle, where the castle is, just at the edge of the middle.

'Just outside the city centre,' Miss Crane says.

I like saying 'edge of the middle' better. It feels more like a place.

Robin Hood came from Nottingham. He lived in Sherwood Forest and formed a merry band of men, including Little John, who was massive. Yorkshire tried to steal Robin Hood. They said he came from there but it's been proven by scientists that he was from Nottingham.

I stopped walking for a minute and looked back at the embankment and the flashing blue lights of the police van.

Sometimes, when I look at the river I imagine it is a long, thin piece of sea. If you followed it for nearly a year, you could reach Australia. It's been here as long as Robin Hood. He might have stood in some of the exact same places as I do, looking at the river. I said that once, to my older brother.

'Course he did,' he replied. 'You daft prat.'

Ryan is my older brother but not a proper one. I've got a different mum and dad to him.

My dad died. I only know him because of the

photographs that Mum kept to show me. I was just a baby then. Miss Crane says our brains store away everything that's happened to us, but you can't remember everything because some memories get locked up in a bit of your brain you don't use, called the 'subconscious'.

In my subconscious, there are pictures and films of my dad playing with me and tucking me into bed. Nobody can take them away and burn them. I wish I could get them out of my locked bit of brain to look at again.

When I got home I stopped at the living-room door on my way upstairs, but nobody turned round. Mum wasn't back from work yet, so I couldn't tell her about what had happened. Sometimes she leaves for work before I wake up and doesn't come back till after I'm in bed, even on the weekends.

Tony was lying on the settee, smoking, with his eyes nearly closed, and Ryan was playing Call of Duty. The gunfire was very loud. Louder than Mum liked it.

Mum says I have to call Tony 'Dad', but secretly, in my head, I always say 'Tony' straight after, so it cancels it out.

Ryan was supposed to go to college to do Media Studies at the beginning of September. After two days he said he didn't like it, so Tony said he could stop going. After that, he played soldier games all day long and nearly all night. When he went up each wave, he went barmy, like he was a real soldier in Afghanistan.

'Yes! Who's the daddy?' he kept saying and punching my arm.

When you say that, it means you think you're the best of anyone in the whole world at something. Ryan thought he was the best at Call of Duty.

'Dean Shelton in my class is on the last wave,' I told him.

'Shut your mouth,' he yelled. 'Before I bleeping smack you one.'

Writing 'bleep' takes all the power out of swear words.

A long, long time ago, someone decided what word to use for every single thing there is. For a wooden thing you sit on, they decided that word would be CHAIR. But what if they had decided it would be called a B*****D? Then you would sit on a B*****D and call someone a CHAIR if you hated them.

'That's true,' Miss Crane had said when I'd asked her about it at school. 'It's the meaning we attach to a word that's important.'

When I've worked at the *Evening Post* for a bit, I want to go and work for Sky.

Sky is 'First for Breaking News'. All the politicians want to talk to Sky first, even before the BBC.

I like Jeremy Thompson but I don't want to present the news like him. I want to do a job like Martin Brunt.

He's my favourite on the Sky News team.

Martin Brunt is the Crime Correspondent. He comes on when very bad stuff happens, like murders. If he lived around here, he would be down at the river now, reporting back to viewers about Jean's friend, who was dead in the water.

The Sky News cameraman would zoom in on the rags and they'd bring criminal experts into the studio to say what kind of person might have killed the man. The experts are called 'criminologists'. They even know what car the murderer drives and whether he still lives with his mum and dad.

In my room, I wrote down all the evidence I'd seen so far in my notebook. I did it in very small writing so I could fit it all in. 'Evidence' means every single thing that has happened. Sometimes on *CSI*, they don't even realize something is evidence until later on. Then they look at their notes to check it out.

I wrote down all the people I'd seen that morning, even Jean. At this stage, everyone was a suspect. Really, I knew Jean hadn't done anything because she used to be a nurse, but sometimes witnesses on Sky News said, 'I can't believe it – she was just an ordinary woman who lived next door.'

Jean doesn't live anywhere. People don't like the homeless; they say they stink and should get a job.

'I'd like to see half of them get a job if they were

starving hungry and freezing cold,' Jean had said, when I'd told her.

Jean used to have a big house in Wollaton with her husband and her son Tim, who wanted to be a pilot. When Tim was killed in a motorbike accident, Jean started to drink so it wouldn't hurt as much. Her husband left her and Jean lost her job.

'I had a mental breakdown,' she said, when we were sitting together on the embankment one day. 'When I got better, I had no husband, no job and no house.'

That's how Jean ended up homeless. It doesn't mean she killed her friend.

The next day, I told Miss Crane all about the homeless man's murder.

'He might have just fallen into the water,' Miss Crane said. 'You mustn't jump to conclusions.'

Falling into the water sounded boring. I felt sure Martin Brunt could find the killer.

I wrote him a letter in class.

Dear Martin Brunt,
There has been a ~~death~~ murder
of a homeless person in our river.
The man was Jean's friend. Can you
come with your cameraman and
bring the Criminology experts?

After I've worked at the Evening
Post for a bit, I want to work with
you at Sky News.
　　Yours sincerely,
　　Kieran Woods
　　Class 9
　　c/o Meadows Comprehensive School,
　　Nottingham

Miss Crane was pleased I'd remembered that it's 'Yours sincerely' when you know someone's name and 'Yours faithfully' when you don't. Before I put the letter in an envelope, I crossed out 'death' and wrote 'murder'.

Miss Crane didn't see me do it.

About the author

Kim Slater honed her storytelling skills as a child, writing macabre tales specially designed to scare her younger brother! Taking her literary inspiration from everyday life, Kim's debut novel, *Smart*, won more than ten regional prizes and has been shortlisted for over twenty regional and national awards, including the Waterstones Children's Book Prize and the Federation of Children's Book Groups Prize. *Smart* was also longlisted for the 2015 CILIP Carnegie Medal. She has written four novels for Macmillan Children's Books set in her home town of Nottingham, where she lives with her husband.

www.kimslater.com

Also by Kim Slater

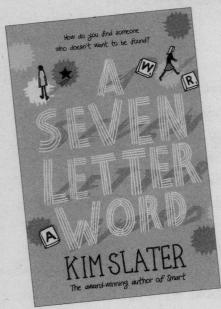

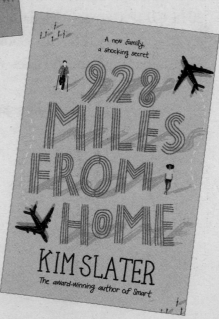